D0438393

The Nancy Drew and the Clue Crew® Collection

#1 Sleepover Sleuths

#2 Scream for Ice Cream

#3 Pony Problems

#4 The Cinderella Ballet Mystery

Join the CLUE CREW & solve these other cases!

#1 *Sleepover Sleuths*

#2 *Scream for Ice Cream*

#3 *Pony Problems*

#4 *The Cinderella Ballet Mystery*

#5 *Case of the Sneaky Snowman*

#6 *The Fashion Disaster*

#7 *The Circus Scare*

#8 *Lights, Camera . . . Cats!*

#9 *The Halloween Hoax*

#10 *Ticket Trouble*

#11 *Ski School Sneak*

#12 *Valentine's Day Secret*

#13 *Chick-napped!*

#14 *The Zoo Crew*

#15 *Mall Madness*

#16 *Thanksgiving Thief*

#17 *Wedding Day Disaster*

#18 *Earth Day Escapade*

#19 *April Fool's Day*

The Nancy Drew and the Clue Crew® Collection

#1 Sleepover Sleuths
#2 Scream for Ice Cream
#3 Pony Problems
#4 The Cinderella Ballet Mystery

By Carolyn Keene

Illustrated by Macky Pamintuan

Aladdin
New York London Toronto Sydney

This book is a work of fiction. Any references to historical events, real people, or real locales are used fictitiously. Other names, characters, places, and incidents are the product of the author's imagination, and any resemblance to actual events or locales or persons, living or dead, is entirely coincidental.

ALADDIN
An imprint of Simon & Schuster Children's Publishing Division
1230 Avenue of the Americas, New York, NY 10020

Designed by Lisa Vega
The text of this book was set in ITC Stone Informal.
Manufactured in the United States of America
This Aladdin edition April 2009
10 9 8 7 6 5 4 3 2 1
Library of Congress Control Numbers:
Sleepover Sleuths 2005931092
Scream for Ice Cream 2005935598
Pony Problems 2005938146
The Cinderella Ballet Mystery 2006920995
ISBN-13: 978-1-4169-9389-6
ISBN-10: 1-4169-9389-4
These titles were originally published individually by Aladdin.

CONTENTS

Chapter One: "Guess What?" 1

Chapter Two: Sleepover Secret 12

Chapter Three: Hello, Dolly! 23

Chapter Four: Cake to Case 29

Chapter Five: Clue Times Two 38

Chapter Six: Hide and Peek 45

Chapter Seven: Party Artie 52

Chapter Eight: Recess . . . Confess 59

Chapter Nine: Picture Perfect 66

Chapter Ten: Detectives Forever! 73

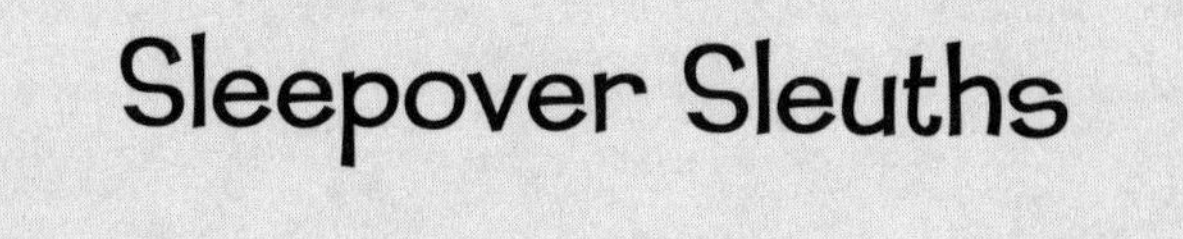
Sleepover Sleuths

CHAPTER ONE

"Guess What?"

"Wow, Nancy," George Fayne said as she raced down the school steps. "I don't know how you do it."

"Do what?" eight-year-old Nancy Drew asked.

"As if you didn't know!" Bess Marvin giggled. She tossed her blond hair as she held her books in both arms. "You guessed the lunch in the school cafeteria again!"

"Oh, that!" Nancy said with a smile.

It was Friday afternoon and Nancy, Bess, and George were leaving River Heights Elementary School. Bess and George were Nancy's two best friends. They were also cousins. The three girls were all in the same third grade class.

They had been friends since kindergarten.

"It was easy to guess," Nancy explained. "The halls smelled fishy today, so that meant we were having fish sticks. And Mrs. Nicholson the lunch lady makes potato salad every three weeks."

"What are we having on Monday?" George quizzed.

"Macaroni and cheese," Nancy replied. "I saw the boxes behind the counter today."

"Yummy!" Bess said. "But I don't want to think about Monday yet."

She glanced at her favorite blue watch. It told the time all over the world. Bess loved all sorts of gadgets. She also loved to build her own.

"It's exactly one minute after three o'clock in the United States," Bess reported. "Which means the weekend has just begun!"

Nancy brushed some reddish-blond hair out of her eyes. "What are you guys doing this weekend?" she asked.

"I'm building a butterfly mobile to hang over my bed," Bess said, her blue eyes flashing.

"There's a neat new game I want to check

out on the computer," George said. "It's called 'Space Cadets from Planet Weirdo'!"

"My cousin, the computer geek!" Bess joked.

"And proud of it!" George declared. "What are you doing this weekend, Nancy?"

"Maybe I'll give Chocolate Chip a bath," Nancy said. "That naughty puppy rolled around in something stinky yesterday—"

"Nancy, Bess, George!" a voice interrupted her.

Nancy and her friends spun around. Deirdre Shannon and her best friend Madison Foley were running across the schoolyard toward them.

Deirdre was in Mrs. Ramirez's class with Nancy, Bess, and George. She was nice, even though Nancy thought she was a bit spoiled. Her mom and dad gave her lots of things. She even had her own Web site, called Dishing with Deirdre. Deirdre wrote about everything on her Web site—from her dance recitals to her dentist appointments!

"Hi, Deirdre," Nancy said. "What's up?"

Deirdre and Madison stopped when they reached the girls. Deirdre tilted her head a little and asked, "Do any of you have a City Girls doll?"

Nancy, Bess, and George traded smiles.

The City Girls were the most awesome dolls ever! Each one came with cool clothes and accessories. And they were each named after a city in the United States.

"I have Chicago Cheryl," Nancy said. "The doll with the purple coat and matching hat. Purple is my favorite color."

Madison nodded at Nancy's purple jacket and sneakers. "As if we didn't know!" she said with a grin.

"I have Oklahoma City Olivia," George added. "She wears the neatest denim outfit and cowboy boots!"

"Honolulu Haley is my City Girl," Bess piped in. "She came with her own little flip-flops and surfboard."

Deirdre rolled her eyes. "I know, I know," she said. "I know all the City Girls. I have five of them myself!"

"Then why did you ask us, *Dee-Dee*?" George asked.

Nancy jabbed George with her elbow. She knew Deirdre hated the nickname Dee-Dee.

"It's *Deirdre*!" Deirdre said.

"How would you like it if we called you *Georgia*?" Madison asked George.

George scrunched her nose when she heard her real name. "No, thanks," she said. "I'll stick with George."

Deirdre reached into her backpack. She pulled out three white envelopes. "Tomorrow night, eight o'clock," she said. "Bring your sleeping bag, toothbrush, and City Girls doll!"

Deirdre handed the envelopes to Nancy, Bess, and George.

Then she and Madison ran across the yard to Kendra Jackson.

"What are these, Nancy?" Bess asked.

"I can't guess everything," Nancy said, smiling. "So there's only one way to find out."

Nancy tore open her envelope and pulled out a card. Her eyes widened as she read the pink writing. It was an invitation to a birthday sleepover on Saturday night!

Bess and George pulled out their own invitations and shrieked.

"Are we lucky or what?" Bess cried. "We have never been invited to any of Deirdre's parties before!"

"Deirdre may be spoiled," George said. "But I'll bet her sleepover will rock our socks!"

Nancy was excited too. Five minutes ago she had zero plans for the weekend. Now she had a cool sleepover to go to with her two best friends!

"This is great," Nancy said. "But I wonder why we have to bring our City Girls."

❀ ❀ ❀

"Toothbrush?" Hannah asked.

"Check!" Nancy answered.

"Flannel pj's with cupcake design?" Hannah asked.

Nancy peeked inside her big purple backpack and smiled. "Check!" she said.

It was seven fifteen on Saturday night. Hannah Gruen was standing in Nancy's lavender and white bedroom, making sure she had everything she needed for the sleepover.

Hannah had been the Drews' housekeeper ever since Nancy's mother died, when she was three years old. Hannah took such good care of her that she was almost like a mother to Nancy.

"Sleeping bag?" Hannah quizzed.

"Sleep?" Nancy cried. "We're not going to sleep, Hannah!"

Hannah raised an eyebrow. "Sleeping bag?" she asked again.

"Check," Nancy said as she tossed her rolled-up sleeping bag on her bed.

"Now, are you sure you have everything?" Hannah asked.

"Sure, I'm sure," Nancy said. She glanced at the clock on her bedside table. "But I'd better go now. Daddy is probably waiting in the car."

Nancy shrugged her backpack over her hoodie. She tucked her sleeping bag under her arm and bounded down the stairs. "I am so totally psyched, Hannah!" she called. "This is going to be the best City Girls party in the—"

Nancy froze on the stairs.

"Oops," she said. "I almost forgot my City Girls doll!"

Hannah stood at the top of the stairs. She pulled Chicago Cheryl from behind her back. "I was wondering how long it would take you to notice!" she said with a laugh.

Nancy tucked Chicago Cheryl under her free arm. She darted out the door and into her dad's car. After they buckled their seatbelts, Mr. Drew drove to the Marvin house to pick up Bess and George. Soon all three girls were sitting in the backseat with their sleepover gear and dolls.

George was wearing all denim, just like Oklahoma City Olivia. Bess wore a little red silk flower in her hair like Honolulu Haley.

"Why does everyone have to bring a City Girls doll to the party?" Mr. Drew asked as he drove.

Mr. Drew was a busy lawyer. But he was never too busy to spend time with Nancy.

"City Girls rule, Daddy!" Nancy said. "Each one is different."

"Anchorage Abby is from Alaska, so she comes with furry boots," Bess said. "And Malibu Marcy has real sand between her toes!"

"That's gross," George said.

"But the most awesome City Girls doll," Nancy said, "is Hollywood Heather!"

"Oooh!" cried Bess.

"Ahhh!" exclaimed George.

There were only a few Hollywood Heathers made in the whole United States. She was very special and very expensive.

"I heard Heather's poncho is made out of real cashmere," Bess said. "That's wool from goats."

"I heard she has real leather boots!" George said.

"And sterling silver earrings!" Nancy put in.

"I read on the City Girls Web site that there's only one Hollywood Heather left in the whole country," George added.

Mr. Drew slowed down as he drove up a tree-lined street. He stopped the car in front of a huge white house.

"This is the Shannon house, girls," Mr. Drew said.

Nancy leaned over Bess and George to look out the window. "Wow!" she exclaimed.

A red carpet lined the path leading to the house. There were huge lights on the lawn and cardboard cutouts of famous movie stars!

Deirdre stepped out of the house wearing dark sunglasses and a fancy feather boa. As Nancy, Bess, and George walked up the red carpet, Mr. Shannon snapped pictures of them. Nancy guessed they were for Deirdre's Web site. Mr. Shannon was a lawyer, just like Nancy's dad.

"Nancy, George, Bess!" Deirdre called, swinging her boa. "Are you ready for your close-up? I mean—sleepover?"

"What's up with this?" Bess whispered to Nancy and George.

"I think Deirdre has gone Hollywood," George whispered.

The flash from Mr. Shannon's camera made Nancy see spots. "I don't get it," she said as she blinked. "Isn't this supposed to be a City Girls party?"

Chapter Two

Sleepover Secret

"Hi, girls!" Mrs. Shannon said as they entered the house. Deirdre's mom was wearing a pink sweater and black stretch pants. Her brown hair was combed in a neat flip.

"Hello," Nancy said in her most polite voice.

"Why don't you bring your gear down to the basement?" Mrs. Shannon said. "That's where the fun is!"

"And the snacks!" Deirdre added.

Deirdre waved them to the door leading to the basement. George pointed to a dark blue duffel bag against the wall. "Looks like someone forgot their bag," she said.

Deirdre squeezed her nose and said, "That's Trina Vanderhoof's smelly basketball bag. I'm making her keep it upstairs so it doesn't stink up the sleepover."

Nancy felt something tickle her ankle. She looked down and saw a furry white cat. It purred softly as it rubbed against Nancy's leg.

"She looks like a marshmallow!" Nancy cooed.

"You guessed her name," Deirdre said. "It's Marshmallow!"

"Can Marshmallow come to the party?" George asked.

"I wish," Deirdre sighed. "Trina is allergic to cats."

Trina Vanderhoof was in Mrs. Bailey's third grade class at school. She was so tall that she played basketball with the fourth grade boys at recess. She was also becoming very good friends with Deirdre.

The girls walked down the narrow staircase to the basement. The room was decorated with silver and gold balloons and big cardboard stars. A sign on the wall read, HOORAY FOR HOLLYWOOD! There was also a big-screen TV, a DVD player, a sofa against one wall, and shelves filled with books and games. A table was piled high with presents for Deirdre.

Nancy saw more girls sitting on the floor with their dolls. She recognized Trina, Kendra Jackson, Madison Foley, Andrea Wu, and Marcy Rubin. Nancy knew everyone from school—except a little girl running around in footsie pajamas.

"Marcy pours orange juice on her cornflakes!" the little girl sang out loud. "Marcy is afraid of spiders!"

"That's my little sister, Cassidy," Marcy groaned. "My parents went to a concert tonight, so I had to bring her."

Cassidy began jumping up and down. "Marcy sleeps with a teddy bear! Marcy bites her toenails—"

"Put a sock in it!" Marcy cut in.

One more girl with copper red hair and freckles

entered the room. It was Nadine Nardo. Everyone knew Nadine wanted to be an actress when she grew up, so her nickname was "Nadine the Drama Queen."

"I love those stars!" Nadine said, pointing to the wall. "They remind me of . . . *me*!"

Nancy, Bess, and George dropped their gear on the floor. They pulled out their birthday presents for Deirdre and placed them on the table with the other gifts. Nearby, on a smaller table, stood something covered with a long white cloth.

"What's under this?" Nancy asked. She was about to lift the cloth when—

"Don't peek! It's a surprise!" Deirdre shouted. She turned to Cassidy, who was creeping toward the table. "Anyone who peeks underneath will grow warts on their nose and hair on their tongue!"

"Pizza time!" Mrs. Shannon sang as she breezed into the room. Behind her Mr. Shannon carried three pizza boxes in his arms.

As the girls sat on the floor to eat their slices, Nancy kept glancing at the small table. "I wonder what's under that cloth," she whispered.

"I hope we find out soon," Bess whispered back.

The girls ate three kinds of pies: pepperoni, mushroom, and extra cheese. Cassidy pressed two pepperonis against her eyes and ran around the room shouting, "I'm an alien from planet Pizza Pie!"

"You mean space cadet," Marcy muttered.

Nancy took a sip of fruit punch. Then she asked, "Where's your City Girls doll, Deirdre?"

"I couldn't decide which one to bring down," Deirdre said with a shrug.

That's a strange excuse, Nancy thought as she picked up another slice.

The girls finished all three pizzas. Then Deirdre opened her presents. She loved the dotted stationery set that Nancy gave her. After all the presents were opened, everyone changed into their pj's and had a pajama fashion show.

"Here is Bess modeling her favorite pink pj's," Nadine announced with a French accent. "Merci, Bess!"

Bess twirled like a supermodel. Then George pretended to walk down a runway in her red and white striped pajamas. Following her was Nancy in her favorite cupcake pj's.

Of all the pajamas, Nadine's orange ones were the brightest. And Nancy thought her slippers with the unicorn heads were the most fun!

"Say cheese!" Deirdre said. She held up her camera. "I want a picture of everyone with their City Girls dolls!"

The girls crowded together. They smiled as they held up their dolls.

"Cheese . . . with pepperoni!" Trina joked.

Deirdre stared at Trina's doll. "What is *that*?" she asked.

"Indianapolis Ivy," Trina answered. "My City Girls doll."

"I know all the City Girls dolls," Deirdre said. "And I never heard of Indianapolis Ivy."

"I've never heard of Indianapolis Ivy, either," Madison said.

"Are you saying my doll is fake?" Trina asked.

Nancy hoped Deirdre and Trina wouldn't fight.

"You guys!" Nancy said. "What difference does it make, as long as we all love our dolls?"

Just then Trina threw back her head and let out a big sneeze. "Ah, ah, ah-choooo!"

"Meeeeow!"

Nancy turned around. She saw Marshmallow the cat padding around the room.

"You know I'm allergic to cats." Trina sniffed.

"My parents must have left the basement door open," Deirdre said. "Sorry, Marshmallow. It's all Trina's fault you can't come to the party." She picked up the cat and carried her up the basement stairs.

Madison giggled. But Trina muttered something like, "Whatever, Dee-Dee."

"Um . . . let's play another game!" Nancy blurted out.

The game they all played was called, "Find the Prize." The girls separated into teams. Then they set out to find a goody bag that Mrs. Shannon had hidden somewhere in the room.

Nancy, Bess, and George were on the same team.

"Where do we start looking?" George asked.

Nancy's eyes darted around the room. She saw something sparkling on the carpet and kneeled down for a closer look. It was a tiny clump of green glitter. A few inches away was another speck of glitter.

"I think I see a trail!" Nancy whispered. "Let's see where it leads."

The girls followed the glitter to a bookshelf. "Look! There's more glitter on one of the shelves," Nancy cried. Tucked between two books was the goody bag—decorated with green glitter!

"Found it!" Nancy called out.

Everyone watched as Nancy opened the goody bag. It was filled with three pink bangle bracelets and three sets of matching barrettes.

"Pretty!" Cassidy exclaimed.

"How did you find it so fast?" Kendra asked.

"Nancy followed the glitter trail!" George said.

"You're good at finding things, Nancy," Andrea said.

"And guessing things," Bess added.

"I guess I am!" Nancy said with a smile.

"You guys!" Deirdre cut in. She was wearing her feathery boa as she stood next to the mystery table. "It's time for my super-big surprise!"

"Yes!" Nancy cheered softly under her breath. They would finally find out what was underneath the cloth!

The girls sat in a semicircle by the table. Deirdre waved her boa and said, "Please welcome . . . the one and only . . . the one of a kind . . . and very expensive . . ."

She whipped off the white drape and shouted, "Hollywood Heather!"

Everyone gasped.

Nancy stared at the doll. Her blond hair hung in curls over her shoulders.

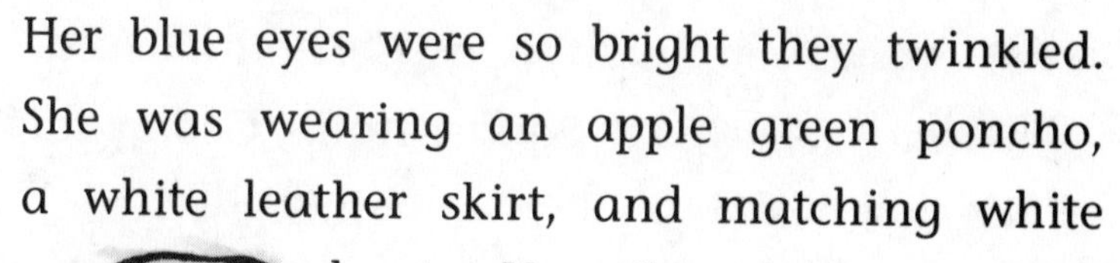

Her blue eyes were so bright they twinkled. She was wearing an apple green poncho, a white leather skirt, and matching white boots. Her silver hoop earrings glowed against her suntanned cheeks.

"It's her!" Nancy swooned.

"It's Hollywood Heather!" Bess sighed.

"That explains the Hollywood party!" Kendra said.

Just then a slipper hit the back wall. Nancy could see it was a unicorn slipper.

"It's not fair!" a voice shouted. "It's not fair!"

CHAPTER THREE

Hello, Dolly!

Nancy recognized the slipper and the voice. Nadine Nardo marched over with her hands planted on her hips. Her bottom lip jutted out in a pout.

"I was saving my allowance for Hollywood Heather!" Nadine said. "I'm going to be a star someday. So I should have Hollywood Heather!"

"Well," Deirdre said, "she's mine."

"Oh, great," George whispered. "This is the second fight so far."

"Why can't we all be friends?" Bess whispered.

"Don't you like your New York Nikki doll?" Nancy asked Nadine. "She has a cool leather jacket and jeans. And her brown hair is so long and shiny."

"Sure, I like her," Nadine said. "But I can have more than one City Girls doll."

"You can play with Hollywood Heather any time, Nadine." Deirdre sighed. She then yelled up the basement stairs, "Mom! Time for cake!"

While the girls admired Hollywood Heather, Nancy looked at Trina and Nadine. They both seemed pretty upset.

"Cake!" Mrs. Shannon sang as she walked in. Mr. Shannon followed. He was carrying a birthday cake glowing with candles. As he set it down everyone smiled. It was decorated with a picture of Hollywood Heather!

After everyone sang "Happy Birthday," Deirdre made a secret wish. Then she blew out the candles. "Let's eat, you guys!" she announced.

The cake tasted as good as it looked. Nancy was enjoying a big piece—until she dropped frosting on her cupcake pajamas!

"Oh, well," Nancy sighed. "Now I have chocolate frosting on my cupcakes."

Soon there was only one piece of cake left. Cassidy was about to reach for it when Deirdre said, "No, you don't. I'm the birthday girl, so I'm saving it for tomorrow."

"Meanie!" Cassidy said, stomping her foot.

After cake everyone painted each other's toenails purple, pink, and blue. A few minutes later, the girls began to yawn.

"We can't fall asleep!" Madison said.

"We're supposed to stay up all night!" Kendra said.

"I guess we have to remember that it's called a *sleepover,*" Nancy said with a yawn, "and not a *wakeover.*"

"I'm putting Hollywood Heather on the windowsill," Deirdre said, "so everyone can see her as we fall asleep."

She carried the doll to the windowsill. Since they were in the basement, the window was much higher than usual—too high for Deirdre to reach.

"Let me do it," Trina said. "I don't play basketball for nothing." She took Hollywood

Heather, reached up, and placed her carefully on the windowsill.

"Thanks," Deirdre said quietly.

"No problem," Trina answered.

The girls lined their gear up against the walls. Then Deirdre snapped a picture of everyone underneath the window.

"It's for my Web site," Deirdre said. "I want the whole world to know I have a Hollywood Heather doll!"

After brushing their teeth and

washing their faces, the girls unrolled their sleeping bags and snuggled inside. Nancy lay between Bess and George. When the lights were out, she could see Hollywood Heather shining in the moonlight.

"It's dark in here!" Cassidy suddenly whined. "No spooky stories, okay?"

"How about some jokes?" George asked in the dark. "Why can't you give a cookie to a teddy bear?"

"Why?" Cassidy's voice asked.

"Because they're always stuffed!" George said.

Some girls laughed. Some groaned.

"My turn," Nancy said. "How do you know if an elephant's been in your refrigerator?"

"How?" Bess asked.

"Because," Nancy said. She could feel her eyelids getting heavier and heavier. "His footprints are in the . . . the . . . the . . ."

That was the last thing Nancy remembered before falling asleep. The next thing she knew, an arm was shaking her awake.

"Where is she?" Deirdre asked in a shaky voice. "Where's Hollywood Heather?"

"Huh?" Nancy asked. She rubbed the sleep out of her eyes. The room was light. The clock on the wall read eight o'clock.

Deirdre was walking between the sleeping bags.

"Where's Hollywood Heather, you guys?" she cried.

Nancy looked at the windowsill. Then she sat straight up. Hollywood Heather was gone!

CHAPTER FOUR

Cake to Case

"What happened to Hollywood Heather?" Nancy asked.

All the girls were wide awake now. They were sitting on their sleeping bags and staring at the window.

"That's funny," George said. "I went to the bathroom at six forty-five this morning. When I came back, the doll was on the windowsill."

"How do you know it was six forty-five?" Bess asked.

"I looked at the clock before I fell back to sleep," George explained.

"Did anyone see what happened to my doll?" Deirdre cried out.

All heads shook back and forth.

"Then help me find her!" Deirdre pleaded.

Nancy scrambled to stand up. She could see that one of the sleeping bags was empty. The basketball design on the bag told her it belonged to Trina.

"Hey, what happened?" a voice asked.

Nancy turned. She saw Trina walk into the room. Trina's eyes widened when Madison told her about the missing doll.

"Look everywhere," Deirdre instructed. "If you find Hollywood Heather, yell out at the top of your lungs!"

The girls searched the room for Hollywood Heather. They looked under tables, behind bookcases—even under sleeping bags. Nancy was about to look near the windows when she saw Cassidy. The little girl sat on top of her sleeping bag. She clutched a yellow and red backpack. The outside flap had a picture of the cartoon character Artie the Aardvark on it.

Why isn't she looking for the doll? Nancy wondered.

"Tell your mom and dad, Deirdre," Kendra said. "Maybe they can help us look."

"I can't!" Deirdre said. "I promised I'd take extra good care of Hollywood Heather."

"It's just a doll," Trina said.

"Just a doll?" Deirdre gasped. "Is the Statue of Liberty just a statue? Is the Great Wall of China just a wall? Is Johnny Appleseed just an apple?"

"He's not an apple," Andrea said slowly. "I think he planted apple trees or something."

"Whatever!" Deirdre cried.

The girls looked for Hollywood Heather for half an hour. But she was nowhere to be found.

"If anyone in this room took Hollywood Heather," Deirdre said, "tell me now."

The room was silent. Then Mrs. Shannon opened the basement door at the top of the stairs and called, "Girls! Breakfast is ready!"

They quietly climbed the stairs. Cassidy was still holding her Artie the Aardvark backpack.

Why is she bringing her backpack to breakfast? Nancy wondered.

Upstairs everyone sat down at the Shannons' dining-room table. Mr. and Mrs. Shannon served scrambled eggs and whole wheat toast. Nancy looked around the table as she ate. Deirdre was picking at her eggs with her fork. Her best friend Madison was pretty quiet too.

As Nancy reached for the strawberry jam, she noticed that Cassidy was leaning over her backpack as she ate.

"Bess, George," Nancy whispered. "Do you think maybe Cassidy took Hollywood Heather?"

"Why do you say that?" Bess asked.

"Cassidy won't let go of her backpack," Nancy said quietly. "And she is sort of a—"

"Pest," George finished.

After breakfast the girls went to the basement to collect their gear.

"Madison," Deirdre asked her best friend. "Can you stay and help me look for Hollywood Heather?"

"Can't!" Madison said quickly. "I have to go home and clean my room."

Deirdre frowned as Madison left the basement. When most of the other girls were gone, she looked sadder than ever.

"Don't worry, Deirdre," Nancy said. "Maybe the person who took Hollywood Heather will give her back soon."

"Sure!" Bess said cheerily. "Nancy even thinks she knows who took her."

"Bess!" Nancy hissed.

"Please tell me, Nancy!" Deirdre said, shaking Nancy's arm. "Who do you think took Hollywood Heather?"

"I don't know for sure," Nancy said. "So I don't want to say anything."

Deirdre looked disappointed. Suddenly her eyes lit up.

"I have a superific idea!" Deirdre said. "Why don't *you* find the person who took Hollywood Heather?"

"Me?" Nancy asked.

"You found the hidden goody bag," Deirdre said.

"And you're great at guessing things, Nancy," George said. "You always guess the school lunch."

"You even guessed Marshmallow's name!" Bess said.

"Yes," Nancy said. "But—"

"Come on, Nancy," George urged. "Don't you want to solve a real-life mystery?"

"You can be like—a detective!" Bess said.

A detective? I am pretty good at finding things and guessing things, Nancy thought. *I do like reading mystery books and watching mystery shows on TV with Daddy. So maybe solving a mystery would be fun . . . way fun.*

"I can try," Nancy said. "But I don't want to do it alone. Does anyone want to help?"

Bess's and George's hands flew up.

"I would if I could," Deirdre said. "But I have to practice my tap, gymnastics, and my recipe for Junior Chefs of America Club today."

"Do *you* think you know who took your doll, Deirdre?" Nancy asked.

Deirdre nodded. "Trina was the only one who could reach the window," she said. "And she came into the basement after the doll was missing. She was probably stuffing Hollywood Heather into her stinky gym bag!"

"But Trina is your friend," Nancy said. "Not your best friend like Madison—but still your friend."

"Maybe she wanted Hollywood Heather more than she wanted to be my friend," Deirdre sighed.

Nancy, Bess, and George stared at Deirdre as she left the basement.

"Wow," George said. "She's totally upset."

"I'm totally psyched," Bess said. "We're going to solve a real-life mystery, you guys!"

The three friends high-fived.

"Now that we're detectives," Nancy said, "where do we start?"

"Don't ask me!" George laughed. "I don't have a clue!"

"Clue!" Nancy exclaimed. "That's it! The first thing we do is look for clues!"

"Let's check the windowsill," Bess said. "That's the last place Hollywood Heather was before she disappeared."

They hurried to the window.

"It is high," George said. "How would a little kid like Cassidy reach the doll?"

Nancy pointed to a bench nearby. "She could have climbed up on that," she said.

The bench wasn't very heavy. The three girls moved it under the window. Then they all climbed up on it. Nancy checked the window to make sure it was locked. It was. Next she ran her hand along the windowsill. Instead of dust, there was some soft white fuzz all over it.

"Maybe it came from Hollywood Heather's

poncho," Bess said. "The wool was soft and fuzzy too."

"It was also green," George said. "This stuff is white."

"Then what is it?" Bess asked.

Nancy examined the wispy fuzz.

"I don't know," she said. "But I think we just found our first clue!"

CHAPTER FIVE

Clue Times Two

"Our first clue!" Bess exclaimed. "How cool is that?"

"Let's take some as evidence," Nancy said.

"Evi-dance? What's that?" Bess asked.

"That's a fancy word for proof," Nancy explained. "My dad explained it to me once when we were watching a mystery movie together."

Nancy tried to pick up the fuzz. But the wisps kept slipping from her fingers.

"Wait here," Bess said as she hopped off the bench. When she came back her hand was wrapped with sticky tape.

"What's that?" George asked.

"A clue mitt!" Bess said. "I built it myself."

Bess ran her sticky mitt over the windowsill. Clumps of fuzz stuck to the tape.

"Thanks, Bess!" Nancy exclaimed.

The girls jumped off the bench. Bess pulled the sticky mitt off her hand. She dropped it into an empty goody bag that she found on a table.

"Let's see what else we can find," Nancy said.

The girls moved the bench. They got down on their hands and knees and searched the cream-colored carpet.

Nancy saw something orange on the floor. She picked it up and rolled it around in her hand.

"It looks like a button," Nancy said. "It might be a clue."

"Two clues!" Bess squealed. "We're on a roll!"

"Now we have to figure out who would have taken Hollywood Heather," Nancy said as she dropped the button into the bag.

"You mean suspects?" George asked.

"How did you know?" Bess asked.

"Nancy isn't the only one who likes mysteries!" George said with a grin.

Nancy looked at the clock. It was almost time for Hannah to pick them up.

"Let's work on the case in my room," Nancy suggested. "We can keep our clues in my desk drawer. And we can use my computer to write down everything we find out."

"Did you say computer?" George said. She gave a thumbs-up sign. "I'm there!"

Bess and George called home for permission to go to Nancy's house. Then Hannah picked the girls up and drove them five blocks to the Drew home.

Nancy, Bess, and George all had the same rules. They had permission to walk up to five blocks as long as they were together. But with all their heavy sleepover gear, five blocks was too far to walk!

As soon as they reached the Drew house, the girls ran straight up to Nancy's room. Nancy carefully placed the clue bag in her top desk drawer. Then she turned on her computer.

George sat down at the keyboard. She opened up a new file and called it "Who Took Hollywood Heather?"

"What do we know so far?" Nancy asked.

"Hmm," George said. "The doll was on the windowsill at six forty-five this morning when I came back from the bathroom."

"Deirdre woke me up at eight," Nancy remembered. "So Hollywood Heather must have disappeared between about seven and eight o'clock in the morning."

"Type that in, George!" Bess said.

"I'm typing! I'm typing!" George said as her fingers flew across the keyboard.

"What about suspects?" Nancy asked.

"We have one already," Bess said. "Cassidy Rubin."

"Right," Nancy said. "Cassidy could have stuffed the doll in her backpack. Maybe that's why she wouldn't let go of it."

"Cassidy was also mad at Deirdre for not letting her have the last piece of birthday cake," George said. "Maybe she took Hollywood Heather to get even."

"That's it. Case closed!" Bess declared. "Cassidy took the doll!"

"We don't know for sure, Bess," Nancy said, shaking her head. "So far she's just a suspect."

George looked up the word "suspect" on the computer's spell-check. She typed it on the page, with Cassidy's name underneath.

"Who else could have taken Hollywood Heather?" Nancy asked.

Bess sat on Nancy's bed. She bounced a stuffed tiger on her lap. "Maybe Deirdre was right about Trina," she said. "Trina *was* mad at her. And she was the only one who could reach the windowsill."

"Anyone could have climbed up on something, though," George said. "Just like we did."

Nancy didn't want to blame Trina. But then she remembered something else. . . .

"Trina's sleeping bag was empty when the doll went missing," Nancy said. "Maybe she did go upstairs to hide the doll in her bag."

George added Trina's name to the suspect list.

"Do you think Trina's doll was a fake, like Deirdre said?" Bess asked.

"Let's check out the City Girls Web site," George said. "They have pictures of all the dolls. Maybe there's a picture of Indianapolis Ivy."

George saved their case file before going online. She was about to search for the City Girls site when she heard a little jingling noise.

"You've got an instant message, Nancy," George said.

Nancy leaned over to read her message. "It's from Pickles99," she said.

"Pickles? Who's that?" Bess asked.

"Brianne Slotsky from school," Nancy explained. "She puts pickles on all her sandwiches."

"Even peanut butter?" Bess gasped.

"Why wasn't Brianne at the sleepover?" George asked. "Doesn't she have a City Girls doll?"

"Not yet," Nancy said. "But that's all she ever thinks about!"

Nancy read the message out loud. "'Nadine called me. She said she has a new Hollywood Heather doll. Is it true?'"

All three girls stared at the message.

"You guys," Nancy said slowly. "Did she just say Nadine has Hollywood Heather?"

Chapter Six

Hide and Peek

"I forgot about Nadine!" George said. "She said Hollywood Heather should belong to her."

"Wasn't Nadine wearing orange pj's?" Bess asked.

"So?" George asked.

"The orange button clue!" Nancy exclaimed. "Good catch, Bess!"

Another message popped up from Pickles99. It said, "Hello? Are you there?"

"I forgot about Brianne!" Nancy said. She quickly typed, "It's news to me. Gotta go!"

"Now we have three suspects," Nancy said as she logged off. "Cassidy, Trina, and Nadine."

"Let's find them," George said. "And tell them we think they took Hollywood Heather!"

"No way, George!" Nancy said. "Good detectives always ask lots of questions before accusing anyone."

"What kind of questions?" Bess asked.

"That's what we have to figure out," Nancy said.

"Can we figure it out over pizza?" Bess asked. "I'm getting hungry."

"You just had scrambled eggs!" George said.

"That was three hours ago," Bess cried.

Nancy printed out their notes.

"A real case file!" she said. "How cool is that?"

Nancy got permission from her dad to go to Pizza Paradise on River Street. Hannah drove Bess and George to their houses to drop off their gear. Then Mrs. Fayne drove the girls to River Street in her van.

Mrs. Fayne owned a catering business. The back of the van was filled with containers of coleslaw and potato salad.

"I have to drop off this food at a bridal shower, girls," Mrs. Fayne said after she parked. "You go straight to the pizza parlor and I'll meet you there at two o'clock."

"Two o'clock?" Bess said. She glanced at her international watch. "Is that two o'clock in England, Italy, or China?"

"Show-off!" George said with a smirk.

Nancy glanced at her own watch. It said one fifteen. That gave them lots of time to eat pizza and talk about the case.

After saying good-bye to Mrs. Fayne, the girls walked up the block to Pizza Paradise. Halfway there Bess grabbed Nancy's arm and whispered, "Don't look now—but look who's there!"

"Bess!" Nancy said. "How can I not look and look at the same time?"

"Then—just look!" Bess whispered.

Nancy looked where Bess was pointing. Standing in front of a grocery store were Nadine Nardo and her mom.

"I don't want Nadine to see us yet," Nancy said quietly. "Let's hide somewhere."

River Street was lined with trees. Nancy, Bess,

and George ducked behind an oak tree with a thick trunk. They were close enough to hear Nadine and her mom talking.

"What you did was not okay, Nadine!" Mrs. Nardo was saying.

"But Mom!" Nadine said. "I had to have a Hollywood Heather doll. I just had to!"

The girls peeked out. Nancy saw Nadine holding a shopping bag at her side. She also saw two doll feet with white boots sticking out at the top.

"You guys," Nancy whispered. "Doesn't Hollywood Heather wear white boots?"

"You bet," George whispered. "If that isn't Hollywood Heather, I'll eat my socks!"

"Gross!" Bess cried.

"Shh!" Nancy said. "We have to see what's in the bag."

Mrs. Nardo went into the grocery store. Nadine stayed out by the gumball machines. She put the shopping bag on the sidewalk as she searched in her waist pack for a quarter.

"Now's our chance," George whispered. "I'm peeking inside that bag!"

"That's snooping!" Nancy said doubtfully.

"We're detectives," George replied. "We're supposed to snoop."

While Nadine put her quarter into the gumball machine, George tiptoed toward her. She grabbed a handle on the shopping bag. But just as she was about to peek inside, a gumball rolled out of the machine onto the sidewalk. Nadine turned to catch it and saw George with her hand on the bag!

"George," Nadine said. "What are you doing?"

Oh, great, Nancy thought.

George froze with her hand on the shopping bag. "Um . . . looking for Hollywood Heather?" she said, looking up at Nadine.

"What?" Nadine cried.

Nancy and Bess ran over.

"First my gumball rolls away and now this!" Nadine stomped her foot. "Do you think *I* took Hollywood Heather?"

"Well," Nancy started to say.

"We know there's a doll in there, Nadine," George said. "Why don't you just let us look?"

Nadine grabbed a handle on the bag. "What are you, some kind of detectives?" she demanded.

"Bingo!" Bess replied with a smile. "How'd you guess?"

Nancy watched as George and Nadine played tug-of-war with the shopping bag.

"We just want to peek!" George insisted.

"You mean sneak!" Nadine said.

The girls kept tugging—until the bag tore in half and Hollywood Heather dropped to the ground! But when Nancy, Bess, and George looked at the doll, they gasped. Her skin was orange, her head had short patches of white hair, and her brown eyes were smudged with colorful gunk!

"Omigosh, Nadine!" Nancy cried. "What have you done to Hollywood Heather?"

Chapter Seven

Party Artie

"Oh, don't have kittens!" Nadine said. She scooped up the doll. "It's not Hollywood Heather!"

"But didn't you tell Brianne Slotsky that you have a Hollywood Heather doll?" Nancy asked.

Nadine heaved a sigh. She touched her forehead with the back of her hand and said, "I wanted Hollywood Heather really badly. So I decided to turn New York Nikki into her."

Nancy, Bess, and George stared at the messy looking doll.

"You mean . . . that's New York Nikki?" George asked, pointing.

Nadine nodded sadly. "A dolly makeover—that was my plan," she said. "I gave her a tan by pouring on my mom's instant tanning lotion. It made her turn orange. I dyed her hair blond with my mom's hair dye. It made her hair break!"

"Wow!" Bess said. "Your mom uses a lot of stuff!"

Nancy cleared her throat. Mrs. Nardo was coming out of the store. "Is everything okay?" she called.

"Can we take New York Nikki to the doll hospital now, Mom?" Nadine asked. "So they can change her back to the way she was before?"

"Yes, Nadine," Mrs. Nardo sighed. "As long as you promise never to give your dolls makeovers again."

Nadine did look sorry for messing up her doll. "Promise," she said. She waved good-bye to Nancy, Bess, and George. Then she followed her mom up the street.

"How do we know that doll wasn't Hollywood Heather?" George asked. "I mean, Nadine could have messed *her* up!"

But as Nancy thought about the doll, something clicked. "That doll's eyes were brown," she said. "Aren't Hollywood Heather's eyes blue?"

"Bright blue!" Bess agreed.

"So that *was* New York Nikki," Nancy said. "Nadine didn't take Hollywood Heather after all."

"Good!" George said. "Now can we please get some pizza? My stomach is rumbling like a runaway roller coaster!"

The girls walked toward Pizza Paradise. Once inside, Nancy and Bess ordered cheese slices. George got pepperoni. They were about to bring their plates to a table when Nancy saw Madison Foley. She was carrying a plate too.

"Do you want to sit with us, Madison?" Nancy asked.

"Can't!" Madison said. "I'm taking my slice to a Pixie Scout meeting."

Then Madison hurried out of the restaurant.

"Madison is in the third grade like us," Bess said. "Don't only first and second graders go to Pixie Scouts?"

"Maybe she got left back for not selling enough cookies," George said with a shrug.

Nancy, Bess, and George sat down at a small round table. They ate their slices and drank water. Suddenly they heard someone yell, "I'm an alien from planet Pizza Pie!"

Nancy glanced up. It was Cassidy Rubin running around the pizza parlor. She was holding pepperonis over her eyes, just like she did at the sleepover.

"Are we lucky or what?" Bess asked. "Cassidy is one of our suspects."

Nancy could see Cassidy's backpack on another table.

"Look!" Nancy said. "There's the backpack she was holding at the sleepover."

"Maybe Hollywood Heather is still inside," Bess said.

"Forget it," George said, shaking her head. "I'm not peeking into any more bags."

"We don't have to peek," Nancy said. "I'll just *feel* the bag to see if there's a doll inside."

"Cassidy won't see you, anyway," Bess said. "She has pepperonis over her eyes."

Nancy stood up and walked quietly to the

other table. She reached over a paper cup for Cassidy's backpack.

"Oops!" Nancy gasped. She had knocked over the paper cup. Purple liquid was spreading across the table!

Nancy didn't want the backpack to get wet, so she quickly picked it up. That's when she heard Cassidy cry, "Help! Nancy Drew is stealing my backpack!"

"No, I'm not," Nancy reassured the younger girl.

Everyone in the pizza parlor was staring at

her, even Mr. and Mrs. Randazzo, the owners.

Cassidy ran over, dragging Marcy by the hand.

"You weren't stealing my sister's backpack, were you, Nancy?" Marcy asked.

"No," Nancy said. She handed the backpack to Cassidy. "I was just trying to find Hollywood Heather."

Marcy stared at Nancy. "My sister may be a pest," she said, "but she's not a thief!"

"Let's ask her," George said. She turned to Cassidy. "Where were you between seven and eight o'clock this morning?"

"That's a weird question to ask a little kid," Marcy said. "She can hardly tell time yet."

"Can so!" Cassidy said. "I was in the living room watching *Artie the Aardvark* on TV. Deirdre's mother said I could."

Nancy smiled. She used to watch *Artie the Aardvark* too, so she knew every cartoon by heart.

"What was the show about, Cassidy?" Nancy asked.

"It was funny!" Cassidy giggled. "Artie was learning how to ride a skateboard in the zoo!"

"What happened?" Nancy asked.

"What are you doing, Nancy?" Bess whispered.

"Who cares about Artie the Aardvark?" George asked.

Nancy kept on listening.

"Artie was riding the skateboard. It flipped over and he fell into the seal pond. Then the seal bounced Artie on his nose like a ball!" Cassidy laughed.

"That's right!" Nancy said.

"I think I get it," George said. "Cassidy knows everything about the show today. So she *was* upstairs watching TV!"

"Not downstairs stealing the doll," Bess added.

But Nancy wasn't totally sure yet.

"One more question, Cassidy," Nancy said. "Why wouldn't you let go of your backpack this morning?"

Cassidy clutched her backpack again. She stared at the floor as she shuffled her feet. "Because," she said, "I did take something!"

Nancy stared at Cassidy. Was it Hollywood Heather?

ChaPTER EiGhT

Recess . . . Confess

"What did you take, Cassidy?" Nancy asked. "Did you take the doll?"

"Yeah, Cassidy," Marcy said. "What's in the bag?"

Cassidy held out her Artie the Aardvark backpack. She lifted the front flap and said, "Stick your hand in and see for yourself."

Nancy reached into the backpack. She felt something mushy and sticky!

"Eww!" Nancy cried. She yanked out her hand. It was dripping with pink and white goo. "What is this stuff?"

"Whipped cream and strawberry filling," Cassidy explained. "After the *Artie the Aardvark* show I was hungry, so I went into the kitchen. I saw the last piece of birthday cake in the refrigerator, but I didn't take it."

"But!" George said. "It's all over Nancy's hand."

"I took it when Mrs. Shannon said I could," Cassidy said. "I didn't want Deirdre to know, so I put the piece in my backpack before everybody woke up."

Nancy held up her drippy hand.

So that's what Cassidy had in her backpack: the last piece of birthday cake!

"I can't eat it now," Cassidy said. "It's too mushy."

"That's for sure," Nancy muttered. She grabbed a stack of napkins to wipe her hand. Then she, Bess, and George left the pizza parlor.

"So far Nadine and Cassidy are innocent," George said. "That means we have only one suspect left."

"Trina Vanderhoof," Bess said.

It was two o'clock. As the girls waited for Mrs. Fayne in front of Pizza Paradise, Nancy was getting worried. What if Trina hadn't taken Hollywood Heather?

What if I never solve the case? Nancy wondered. *What will I tell Deirdre?*

"It's not easy being a detective, Daddy," Nancy said that night at dinner. "I have only one suspect left."

Mr. Drew wasn't a detective, but he was a lawyer. So he knew a thing or two about cases.

"Sometimes clues can lead to other clues, Pumpkin," Mr. Drew said as he buttered his roll.

"How?" Nancy asked.

Mr. Drew winked at Nancy and said, "I have a feeling you'll find out for yourself."

"I sure hope so, Daddy." Nancy sighed.

After dinner Nancy helped Hannah dry the

dishes. As she dried the last glass, the phone rang. Nancy put the towel on the counter and picked up the kitchen phone.

"Hello?" she said.

"Did you find my doll?" Deirdre's voice asked.

"Um . . . not yet, Deirdre," Nancy answered slowly.

"You have to find her by tomorrow afternoon!" Deirdre wailed. "My father is taking me to tea after school. He told me to bring Hollywood Heather!"

"You still didn't tell your parents that she's missing?" Nancy asked.

"I can't!" Deirdre said.

Nancy chewed her lower lip. It was already Sunday night. They would be in school the whole day on Monday. When would she work on the case?

"I still have to talk to Trina," Nancy said.

"Then go straight to Trina tomorrow and ask her where she hid my doll," Deirdre said. "Or look inside her basketball bag. Just be sure to hold your nose first!"

"I'll do the best I can, Deirdre," Nancy promised. She could hear Deirdre groan on the other end.

"First my doll disappears," Deirdre said. "Then my best friend Madison has no time for me. . . . My life is so hard!"

Nancy heard a click. Deirdre had hung up the phone. Nancy pressed the off button on the phone and turned around. Chocolate Chip was sitting behind her. The little brown puppy cocked her head as she looked up at Nancy.

"Wow, Chip," Nancy said. "Being a detective is a lot harder than I thought!"

"I still can't believe we have to solve the case by this afternoon!" George cried.

"That's just a few hours from now," Bess said. "How are we going to do that, Nancy?"

Nancy shook her head. It was Monday. The third and fourth graders were in the schoolyard for recess. Most of the kids were playing kickball. Some were on the swings. Others were shooting hoops on the basketball court.

"Deirdre wants me to question Trina today,"

Nancy said. "But I don't want to embarrass her in front of everybody."

"Me neither," Bess said.

"She also wants us to look inside her basketball bag," Nancy said.

"Nuh-uh!" George groaned. "That is one bag I'm definitely not looking into!"

"Did you bring our clues to school, Nancy?" Bess asked. "Maybe we can check them out some more."

Nancy pulled the plastic clue bag from her jacket pocket. Inside were the fuzzy tape and the orange button.

"My dad says that clues can lead to other clues," Nancy said. "But I still don't know what he means."

She dropped the bag back into her pocket. Just then a basketball rolled against her foot. Nancy looked up and saw Trina standing on the basketball court. Next to her stood Ned Nickerson from the fourth grade.

Nancy and Ned went to the same pediatrician. They used to play in the waiting room together when they were little.

"Throw it here, Nancy!" Trina called.

"Yeah, Nancy," Ned called. "Give it your best shot!"

"Okay," Nancy said with a smile. She picked up the ball. She was about to toss it when someone snatched it out of her hands.

"Hey!" Nancy said.

She turned and saw Deirdre clutching the ball. Her mouth was a grim line as she stared across the schoolyard at Trina.

"You're not getting it back, Trina Vanderhoof!" Deirdre shouted. "Not until you answer all of Nancy's questions!"

ChaPTER NiNE

Picture Perfect

"What do you want to ask me, Nancy?" Trina asked as she walked over. "Go ahead. Spill."

Nancy opened her mouth but nothing came out.

"How come you left the basement yesterday morning when my doll disappeared?" Deirdre blurted out.

"I had to," Trina said. "My nose was getting all tickly. Someone must have let Marshmallow in."

"I may have left the door open when I went to the bathroom," George said. "My bad."

"It's okay," Trina said. She raised an eyebrow at Deirdre. "Hey. You don't think I took Hollywood Heather, do you?"

Deirdre stared back at Trina. She tossed the

basketball back at her and said, "Ask Nancy. She's the detective."

Nancy's jaw dropped as Deirdre ran away. She also saw Madison standing nearby. Madison was watching Deirdre as she ran away.

"Nancy?" Trina asked. "Do *you* think I stole Hollywood Heather?"

Nancy turned to Trina. She took a deep breath and said, "We thought you might have because you were out of the room. And you were the only one who could reach the windowsill."

"Oh," Trina said.

"And we found clues near the window," George said. "Show her, Nancy!"

Nancy took out the plastic clue bag. "We found an orange button and some fuzzy stuff on the windowsill."

"We're detectives now," Bess said. "In case you haven't noticed."

Trina stared through the clear bag. She frowned, stepped back, and said, "I know what that fuzzy stuff is!"

"What?" Nancy asked.

Trina opened her mouth to speak when—

"Hey, Trina!" Ned called. "We're waiting for the ball!"

"I'm there!" Trina answered. As she ran back to the court, she shouted over her shoulder, "And I didn't take Hollywood Heather!"

Then who did? Nancy wondered as she watched Trina jog toward the boys. Nancy noticed that Madison had disappeared.

"I believe Trina left because of Marshmallow," Bess said. "But why do you think she looked so weird when she saw the fuzzy stuff in the bag?"

"Yeah!" George chuckled. "You'd think she saw a cat!"

Cat. Nancy thought. *That's it!*

"Isn't Marshmallow a white cat?" Nancy asked.

Bess and George both nodded.

"And don't most cats like to sit on windowsills?" Nancy asked.

Her friends nodded again.

"Maybe Marshmallow came into the room, jumped from the gift table to the windowsill, and knocked down Hollywood Heather!" Nancy said.

"Okay," George said. "But wouldn't Hollywood Heather have fallen down somewhere?"

"We did look everywhere for the doll," Bess said. "So where did she fall?"

"That's the big question," Nancy sighed.

The school bell rang. Recess was over. Nancy, Bess, and George walked to the door with the other kids.

"Maybe there's still time to talk about the case after school," Bess said.

"Yeah," George agreed. "I already got permission to go to your house at three o'clock."

"Me too!" Bess said.

"Okay," Nancy said. "But time is running out."

They filed into Mrs. Ramirez's classroom. As Nancy sat at her desk, she tried not to look at Deirdre. She tried not to think about the case, but it kept popping into her head!

Where is Hollywood Heather? Nancy wondered. *Why can't I figure it out?*

After school the girls went to Nancy's house. After eating a snack of Hannah's yummy fruit salad, they went upstairs to Nancy's room. This time Nancy sat at the computer. Instead of opening the case file, she went online.

"There's got to be a site for junior detectives," Nancy said. "Maybe it has some tips on solving cases."

"Wait," George said. She pointed to the little red mailbox on the screen. "You got an e-mail."

Nancy clicked on the mailbox. Her e-mail was from KJack—Kendra Jackson. She wrote: "Check out Deirdre's Web site. There are some neat pictures of all of us!"

Nancy found Dishing with Deirdre on the Web. There were lots of pictures from the sleepover. The girls smiled when they saw the group photo.

"Look!" Bess said. "There's Hollywood Heather on the windowsill before she disappeared."

Nancy gazed at the picture. There were lots of backpacks and duffel bags against the wall too.

"You guys," Nancy said. She leaned forward in her chair. "Could Hollywood Heather have fallen into a bag?"

"Maybe," Bess said. "But which one?"

George squeezed next to Nancy on the chair. She grabbed the mouse and clicked on the picture. Soon the picture was three times its original size!

Nancy studied the photo. She saw flashes of orange between everyone's feet. Maybe there was an orange bag under the window. Nancy pulled out the orange button and held it against the screen. They were the exact same color!

"I think this button came from the bag we

can see in the picture!" Nancy exclaimed. "But who had an orange bag at the sleepover?"

"Can't remember," Bess said, shaking her head.

"Let's check the other pictures," George said. She found shots of the guests walking to the house. One was of Madison carrying an orange duffel bag. It had orange buttons on the front flap!

"Madison's bag was under the window," Bess said.

Nancy couldn't take her eyes off the picture.

"Omigosh!" she gasped. "Does Deirdre's best friend have Hollywood Heather?"

Chapter Ten

Detectives Forever!

"But Madison is Deirdre's best friend, Nancy," Bess said. "If she found the doll, she would have told Deirdre."

"Unless Madison didn't want to tell her," Nancy said. "Let's go to Madison's house and ask her some questions. Anyone know where she lives?"

"She lives in that big blue house on Acorn Street," Bess said. "But I don't know how to get there from here."

"Piece of cake!" George said. With a few clicks of the mouse she found a site called Map Search. In a few seconds a map of River Heights was on the screen.

"Acorn Street is only four blocks away," Nancy said.

"We're allowed to walk there as long as we're together," Bess said, repeating their rules.

George printed out the map. "See?" she said. "There isn't anything you can't find on the computer!"

The girls asked Hannah's permission to go. Then they followed the map to the Foley house. Once there, Nancy rang the doorbell. Madison looked surprised when she opened the door.

"Hi," Madison said. "What's up?"

"Madison, did you find Hollywood Heather in your orange duffel bag?" Nancy asked.

Madison's eyes opened wide. She stepped outside and shut the front door behind her. "No way!" she said.

"Okay," Nancy said slowly. "Then did you lose a button?"

She pulled the orange button out of her pocket. Madison stared at it and said, "Maybe. So what?"

"We think Marshmallow the cat knocked Hollywood Heather off the windowsill," Nancy explained. "And since your bag was right under the window . . ."

". . . accidents happen," Bess finished.

Madison stared at the girls.

"It *was* an accident!" she finally said. "I found the doll in my bag when we were searching the room. I was going to tell Deirdre, but she seemed so mad. She would have thought I stole Hollywood Heather for sure!"

"But Deirdre's your best friend," George said.

"That's just it," Madison said. "I was afraid she wouldn't be my best friend anymore. And that would be awful!"

"So you let Deirdre think that Trina did it?" Bess asked.

When Madison heard Trina's name, she frowned. It made Nancy think of something else.

"Unless you were a little jealous of Trina," Nancy said gently. "For becoming Deirdre's second-best friend."

"I guess I was feeling a little sad about it," Madison said.

Nancy felt bad for Madison. It must have been superhard to keep such a big secret.

"But I still can't tell," Madison said, shaking her head. "Deirdre's dad is a big-shot lawyer. He could throw me into jail for stealing!"

"Nancy's dad is a lawyer too," Bess said with a smile. "He could get you out!"

"No one is going to jail, you guys!" Nancy said. "We can help explain everything to Deirdre."

"It's not that easy," Madison said. "There's another problem."

"What?" Nancy asked.

Madison ran into the house. She came back holding Hollywood Heather. Nancy looked at the doll. One of her arms was missing!

"How did that happen?" Nancy asked.

"It must have broken off when she fell into my bag," Madison said. She held up the broken arm. "How can I bring her to Deirdre like this?"

"Give her to me," Bess said.

Madison handed the doll to Bess. Everyone watched as Bess popped the arm right back in.

"How did you do that?" Madison gasped.

"Bess can build anything and fix anything," Nancy said cheerfully. "Now let's all go to Deirdre's house."

Deirdre lived around the corner from Madison. Mrs. Shannon greeted the girls and led them into the living room. Madison held Hollywood Heather behind her back as they waited for Deirdre.

When she came into the room, Deirdre was wearing a pink dress and black patent leather shoes.

"Hi," Deirdre said. "I'm going to tea soon—"

Madison pulled the doll out from behind her back. Deirdre took one look at it and her mouth dropped open.

"You found her!" Deirdre cried. She grabbed Hollywood Heather from Madison and held her tight. "Where was she?"

"I . . . I . . . I," Madison started to say.

"It's okay, Madison," Nancy whispered.

Madison took a deep breath. "Hollywood Heather fell into my bag," she blurted. "I didn't tell you because I thought you'd think I took her on purpose."

Deirdre stared at Madison. But then she smiled. "So *that's* why you've been too busy for me," Deirdre said. "Thanks for telling me the truth, Madison."

"So . . . you're not mad?" Madison asked.

"I'm just happy you're still my friend," Deirdre said. "Ever since Hollywood Heather went missing, you've been running away from me. I thought I did something wrong!"

"Sorry," Madison said. "But if it weren't for Nancy, I probably wouldn't have had the courage to say anything."

"I knew Nancy would find Hollywood Heather," Deirdre said.

"You mean Nancy, Bess, and George!" Nancy said.

Deirdre hugged Hollywood Heather. "Now I can take Hollywood Heather to tea with me," she said. "Just like my dad said I should."

Then she looked up and said, "Why don't you *all* come to tea? There'll be sandwiches and little cakes and minty tea—"

"I love little cakes!" George said.

"And big cakes!" Bess said, licking her lips.

It sounded good to Nancy, too. But she wanted Deirdre and Madison to fix up their friendship together.

"Thanks, Deirdre," Nancy said. "But we have to go home."

"I know!" Madison said. She turned to Deirdre and smiled. "Let's ask Trina to come with us. She's our second-best friend."

"Okay!" Deirdre said. "And guess what?"

"What?" everyone asked at the same time.

"There *is* a City Girls doll called Indianapolis Ivy," Deirdre said. "So I was wrong and Trina was right!"

Deirdre and Madison walked Nancy, Bess, and George to the door. As the three friends left the house, Madison called after them, "You guys should solve more mysteries. You're great at it!"

Walking down Acorn Street, Nancy thought about what Madison said. Maybe she was right. . . .

"You guys," Nancy said. "Maybe we *should* solve more mysteries!"

Bess and George stopped walking.

"You mean like a team?" George asked.

"Like a *club*!" Nancy said excitedly. "We can meet in my room to talk about our cases. And we can put all of our clues in my desk drawer just like we did for this case!"

"And I can write everything on your computer!" George said, her dark eyes flashing. "That was awesome!"

Bess gave a little excited hop. "And I can fix whatever breaks," she said. "And build some neat spy gadgets, too."

Nancy smiled. Their new detective club was

sounding better and better. But one thing was missing. Something very important . . .

"We need a name," Nancy said. "How about . . . the Mystery Girls?"

"Too old-fashioned," George admitted. "How about . . . Case Crackers?"

"We'd sound like a crunchy snack!" Nancy giggled.

"Let's see," Bess said. She twirled a lock of her hair as she thought. "What about . . . the Clue Gang?"

"Hmm," Nancy said. "Something that rhymes might be nice."

"Like what?" George asked.

"Like the Clue . . . the Clue . . ." Nancy started to say. Her eyes lit up. "The Clue Crew!"

The girls high-fived.

"Our own detective club!" Bess cried. "How cool is that?"

"Supercool!" Nancy agreed. "But do you want to know the best part?"

"We're going to be solving all kinds of cool cases?" George asked.

"No," Nancy said.

"What?" Bess asked.

"We're going to be solving all kinds of cool cases . . . *together*!" Nancy said with a smile.

Nancy Drew and the Clue Crew could hardly wait!

Head-To-Toe PJ Fashion Show!

Go glam at your next sleepover with a pajama fashion show! But before you strut down the runway in your favorite pj's, top off the look—and the fun—with hats made by you and your friends!

Get started with these cool chapeaus . . .

1. Hearts and Flowers Crown:

You will need:

1 paper plate
Construction paper
Paint, markers, or crayons
Scissors
Glue

Cut a slit down the middle of the paper plate. Leave about an inch around the edges of the plate. Cut three more slits the same size. These slits should cross the first one. Bend the points out to look like a crown. Using glue—and your imagination—attach paper hearts and flowers to points and sprinkle with glitter all around. You glow, girl!

2. Paper Bag Hat

You will need:

1 large paper grocery bag

Scissors

Stapler

Markers or crayons

Glue

Feathers, ribbon, buttons, glitter, etc.

Draw a hat shape on the grocery bag. Cut out two of the shapes. Staple two pieces together. Using glue, go wild with feathers, ribbons, glitter—whatever you want to decorate! From supermarket to supermodel—your grocery bag hat will rule the runway!

Now you're ready to wear it . . . and work it!

Jump into history!
Read all the books in the

series!

#1 Lincoln's Legacy

#2 Disney's Dream

#3 Bell's Breakthrough

#4 King's Courage

#5 Sacagawea's Strength

Coming Soon:

#6 Franklin's Fame

Nancy Drew and the Clue Crew

#2

Scream for Ice Cream

By Carolyn Keene

Illustrated by Macky Pamintuan

Aladdin Paperbacks
New York London Toronto Sydney

CONTENTS

CHAPTER ONE: WHAT'S THE SCOOP 1

CHAPTER TWO: KENDRA'S SECRET 9

CHAPTER THREE: BACKPACK ATTACK 17

CHAPTER FOUR: SUPERMARKET SURPRISE! 28

CHAPTER FIVE: STICKS AND CONES 37

CHAPTER SIX: CLUB FLUB 44

CHAPTER SEVEN: CANDY-HANDED 52

CHAPTER EIGHT: ICE SCREAM! 61

CHAPTER NINE: WHAT'S FOR DESSERT? 70

CHAPTER TEN: CHOCO-LATE! 79

CHAPTER ONE

What's the Scoop?

"Can we taste the ice cream now?" Bess Marvin asked.

George Fayne rolled two doubled-up coffee cans on top of the picnic table. The middle can was filled with very cold milk, sugar, vanilla, and blueberries. "I told you a gazillion times, Bess," she said. "Not until it's ready!"

"Unless you want mushy ice cream," eight-year-old Nancy Drew said with a giggle.

Bess and George were Nancy's two best friends. They were cousins, too, but as different as strawberry and fudge ripple ice cream. George was really into computers. Bess could fix or build anything—like the homemade ice-cream maker

George found instructions for on the Web.

Nancy had been counting the days until Saturday. That's when the new Jim and Barry's Ice Cream Factory would open on River Street. It was also the day of the Jim and Barry's ice-cream flavor contest. Whoever came up with the best flavor would win a special silver ticket. The ticket would allow the winner to come into the factory any time for a free pint of ice cream!

The thought of Jim and Barry's ice cream always made the girls' mouths water. They had neat flavors like Squirrel Nut Crunch, Gorilla Vanilla, and Cookie Crumble!

For the contest, Nancy, Bess, and George came up with a flavor called Clue-berry. It was vanilla ice cream loaded with blueberries and a secret surprise—like a big juicy strawberry on the bottom.

"The best part," Nancy said, "is the clues on each container leading to the surprise!"

"It's like a mystery in every pint!" George declared.

"And everybody knows we *love* mysteries!" Bess exclaimed.

That's because Nancy, Bess, and George were great at solving mysteries. They had even started their own detective club called the Clue Crew. Their detective headquarters were in Nancy's room. They carefully kept their clues in Nancy's desk drawer. George wrote their detective files on Nancy's computer.

"Can we taste it now?" Bess asked, twirling a lock of her blond hair around her finger.

"Not until it's ready!" Nancy and George said together.

Just then the sound of bells filled the air. Nancy would know that sound anywhere—it was the jingle of the Mr. Drippy ice-cream truck.

"If you want ice cream so badly, Bess," George said, "why don't you buy some from Mr. Drippy?"

"Mr. Drippy?" Bess answered. She gave a little shudder. "I'd rather buy ice cream from Godzilla!"

"Mr. Drippy *is* Godzilla," Nancy said. "He's the meanest ice-cream man in River Heights. Maybe the world!"

The truck pulled up to the sidewalk. Three kids walked over to it. Mr. Drippy leaned out of the square window on the truck. Without a smile he began to bark, "Fall in line! Heads up! First customer—go!"

The first boy in line wore a baseball cap and a very worried look on his face. "Um," he gulped, "Panda Bar."

Mr. Drippy narrowed his eyes. "No please, no Panda Bar!" he declared. "*Next*!"

A girl in a white T-shirt and red shorts marched up to the window. She threw back her shoulders and shouted, "One chocolate ice-cream pop, please, *sir*! Thank you, *sir*!"

Mr. Drippy nodded as he handed the girl the pop.

"See?" Bess whispered. "Mr. Drippy doesn't give ice cream to anyone who forgets to say please or thank you!"

Nancy saw a boy inside the truck. It was Henderson, Mr. Drippy's son. Henderson was in the fourth grade at River Heights Elementary

School. He was also the biggest brat in school!

"Henderson probably never says please or thank you," Nancy said. "And he must get all the ice cream he wants."

"Forget it," George said. "If we win this contest we won't ever have to buy ice cream from Mr. Drippy again."

As the truck pulled away from the curb, Henderson leaned out

the window. "What's the matter, girls?" he sneered loudly. "Don't you like ice cream?"

"We don't like you," George muttered under her breath.

"At least Jim and Barry are nice," Bess said.

Nancy brushed a wisp of her reddish blond hair from her forehead. "Guess what? My dad read in a newspaper that Jim and Barry will be at the factory tomorrow," she said. "That's when we're supposed to sign up for the contest!"

"I'll be there too!" a voice said.

Nancy, Bess, and George turned their heads. Deirdre Shannon was walking into the yard. Deirdre was in the girls' third-grade class at school. She usually got whatever she wanted—like her own Web site, called Dishing with Deirdre.

"Hi, Deirdre," Nancy said. "We're making ice cream!"

"What a cowinky-dink!" Deirdre said. She held up a small red notebook. "I'm writing about the contest. So I have to taste everybody's ice cream. It's called research."

George tossed her dark curls as she laughed. "You mean it's called getting to eat a ton of ice cream!" she teased.

"Ha, ha," Deirdre said with a frown.

"Our ice cream isn't ready yet, Deirdre," Nancy said. "But Hannah has a pitcher of lemonade in the kitchen."

Hannah Gruen was the Drews' housekeeper. She had been taking care of Nancy since Nancy's mother died when she was only three years old. Hannah cooked the best vegetable lasagna, baked the best cookies, and gave Nancy the best hugs in the whole world.

"Will Hannah give me one of her famous oatmeal cookies, too?" Deirdre asked, her eyes flashing.

"If you say please!" Nancy said.

"I'm there!" Deirdre said, running toward the house.

"Wow," George said. She stopped rolling to

shake out her hand. “My hand hasn’t been this tired since I instant-messaged my pen pal in California for an hour.”

“An hour?” Bess cried. “You call that instant?”

Suddenly Nancy heard a rustling noise. She thought it was a squirrel in the hedge until she heard a girl’s voice hiss, “Nancy! Bess! George!”

“Who’s there?” Nancy hissed back.

A girl slowly stood up behind the hedge. It was their friend Kendra Jackson. Her shiny black hair was tied back in a tight ponytail. She wore a pair of black sunglasses. She looked very mysterious. She looked like a spy!

“Hi, Kendra,” Nancy said. “What’s—”

“Shhhhh!” Kendra said, putting her index finger to her lips. “I need you to keep a secret . . . a TOP SECRET!”

Chapter Two

Kendra's Secret

"We're good at keeping secrets," Nancy said.

"We're detectives," George said. "Secrets are our business!"

Kendra walked into the yard. She was holding a blue and white picnic cooler by the handle. "I know," she said. "That's why I picked you guys to share my secret with."

Bess bounced up and down on the bench. "I love secrets!" she squealed. "What is it? What is it?"

Kendra placed the cooler on the table. She lifted the lid. Nancy looked inside and saw a white Styrofoam container.

"It's my flavor for the contest,"

Kendra explained. "I made it with my grandfather's old ice-cream maker."

"Why did you bring it here?" Nancy asked.

"I need another opinion," Kendra answered. "My mom and dad love it, but parents always love everything their kids do."

Nancy watched as Kendra pulled the lid off the container. The ice cream inside was dark brown.

"I call it Chock Full of Chocolate," Kendra said. "It has chunks of chocolate inside. Four *kinds* of chocolate."

"Four?" Bess asked.

"I can only think of two," Nancy said.

Kendra laid the container on the table. She

gave the girls each a plastic spoon. "Ready, set, go!" she said.

Nancy stuck her spoon inside the container and into her mouth. She felt the ice cream melt on her tongue. The chocolaty flavors exploded in her mouth like fireworks!

"Well?" Kendra asked. "What do you think?"

Nancy swallowed and said, "Three words: OH MY GOSH!"

George was still chewing on a chocolate chunk when she said, "This ice cream is awesome!"

"It's super-awesome!" Bess said.

Kendra gave a little jump. "Do you think it's a winner?" she asked.

"What's a winner? What's a winner?"

All four girls spun around. Standing a few feet away and holding an oatmeal cookie was Deirdre.

Kendra stared at Deirdre with wide eyes. She turned to her cooler and shut the lid. "I've got to go," she said.

"Wait, Kendra! I know you

told Nancy, Bess, and George something," Deirdre said. She turned to the girls and said, "She did—didn't she?"

"Um," Nancy said.

"Er," George said.

Bess shrugged and said, "Only because we're good at keeping secrets!"

Nancy and George glared at Bess. She was sometimes better at keeping secrets than keeping her mouth shut!

"Since when am I *not* good at keeping secrets?" Deirdre asked Kendra.

"Since you spilled the beans about Marcy Rubin's surprise party," Kendra said. "And the time you told me what I'd be getting from my Surprise Santa at school. . . ."

"Don't forget the time you told everybody my real name," George said.

"Give me a break! Everybody knows your real name is Georgia!" Deirdre said. She turned to Kendra. "Tell me your secret, Kendra. Please? Pretty please? With sugar on top?"

Kendra took a deep breath. Then she said,

"Okay, Deirdre. I invented a flavor for the ice-cream contest."

"Cool! What's in it?" Deirdre asked.

"Can't tell you," Kendra said. "Not that you'd steal it, but you might tell people about it on your Web site."

Deirdre's lower lip jutted out. Her face turned red.

They can't have a fight, Nancy thought. *Kendra and Deirdre are good friends!*

"I know, Deirdre," Nancy said. "Why don't you *promise* Kendra you won't write her recipe on your Web site."

Deirdre turned to Kendra. "I won't write your recipe on my Web site," she said. "Cross my heart and hope to croak—drop an eyeball in my Coke!"

"In that case," Kendra said. She lifted the lid of the cooler and pulled out the ice-cream container. "It's called Chock Full of Chocolate. It has four kinds of chocolate—"

Deirdre wasn't listening. She grabbed a spoon, stuck it into the ice cream, then put it into her mouth. The girls watched as Deirdre's eyes popped wide open. Right away she began licking every drop of ice cream off her spoon.

"I'll take a wild guess and say you like it," George said.

"Are you serious? I totally love it!" Deirdre cried. "Chock Full of Chocolate is the real deal!"

"Remember, Deirdre," Kendra said. "You promised."

"Your secret is safe with me," Deirdre said.

Kendra smiled.

"Good," she said. "Who wants to come to my house and see my grandfather's ice-cream maker? He used to make ice cream on the porch with his own grandpa when he was a kid!"

"They had ice cream in those days?" Deirdre asked. "This I've got to see!"

Nancy, Bess, and George decided not to go. They still had a pint of ice cream to make. The Clue Crew said good-bye to Kendra and Deirdre as the two friends left the Drews' front yard.

"I'm glad they're still friends," Nancy said.

Bess was twisting her hair nervously. "What

if Kendra's ice cream is better than Clue-berry?" she asked.

"There's one way to find out," George said. She lifted the lid off their coffee-can ice-cream maker. The ice cream inside wasn't rock hard, but it was firm enough to taste.

One by one the girls tasted their Clue-berry ice cream.

"It's good!" Nancy said.

"But it's not Chock Full of Chocolate." Bess sighed.

"Maybe we should hide a strawberry *and* a chunk of chocolate on the bottom," George suggested.

"Or maybe we should just hope we win," Nancy said.

"I have an idea, Nancy," Mr. Drew said. "Let's have some of your ice cream for dessert."

It was early evening. Nancy's father was barbecuing in the backyard. Mr. Drew was a lawyer. He liked helping Nancy with her Clue Crew cases. He also liked barbecuing in his favorite stain-splattered red and white checked apron.

"Sorry, Daddy," Nancy said. "Our ice cream is for the contest this Saturday."

Mr. Drew pretended to look hurt.

"But don't worry," Nancy said. "If we win the contest, we'll have a different Jim and Barry ice cream every week!"

Hannah walked over carrying a bowl of fruit salad with walnuts. Nancy's Labrador retriever puppy, Chocolate Chip, jumped after her.

"What about my desserts?" Hannah asked. "Those guys will put me out of business!"

Nancy wrapped her arms around Hannah's waist and gave her a big hug. "That will never happen, Hannah," she said. "Your desserts rock!"

The cordless phone on the patio table rang. Nancy ran to answer it. "Hello?" she asked.

"Sh-she did it!" Kendra's voice stammered. "I told you she'd do it—and she did it!"

"Who did what, Kendra?" Nancy asked.

"Deirdre!" Kendra said. "She broke her promise!"

CHAPTER THREE

Backpack Attack

"No way!" Nancy gasped. "Did Deirdre write your secret recipe on her Web site?"

"No," Kendra answered. "But she did write that I had a winning recipe."

"What's wrong with that?" Nancy asked.

"Don't you see?" Kendra asked. "Now all the kids in the conest will want to steal my secret recipe!"

Nancy shook her head, even though she knew Kendra couldn't see her do it over the phone. "They can't do that unless you *tell* them your recipe," she said. "Besides, most of the kids we know are honest."

"Yeah," Kendra snorted. "Until they want to win free ice cream!"

Click!

Kendra had hung up. But Nancy wasn't worried. Tomorrow they would all sign up for the contest. It would be so exciting that Kendra would forget about Deirdre's Web site.

Nancy reached down to scratch Chocolate Chip behind her floppy little ears. "And may the best ice cream win!" she declared.

"There it is," Bess said, pointing. "Is that the most awesome building you ever saw in your whole life?"

"And just think," Nancy said. "It's filled with the yummiest ice cream in the whole wide world!"

It was Thursday morning. Hannah had driven Nancy, Bess, and George to the Jim and Barry's Ice Cream Factory. A huge crowd of kids stood in front of the factory, all set to sign up for the ice-cream flavor contest.

Nancy could see a stage set up in front of the factory. Purple, yellow, and white balloons swept over the stage in an arch.

"If this is just for the sign-up," Nancy said, "I can't wait to see what they do for the contest!"

"I'm going down the street to buy some fruits and vegetables," Hannah said. "Stay here and stay together."

Nancy, Bess, and George nodded. The friends all had the same rules. They could walk or ride their bikes five blocks from their houses as long as they were together. Anywhere farther than that, they had to be driven by a parent or Hannah.

"And if you get any free ice-cream samples," Hannah said with a wink, "save one for me!"

Nancy hugged Hannah good-bye. Then the three excited friends joined the crowd. Music blared from loudspeakers as kids from the River Heights Dance School tapped across the stage in ice-cream cone costumes. Nancy saw their friend Nadine Nardo dancing with the group.

Nadine wanted to be an actress and loved being on stage. But today she was frowning as her ice-cream hat began tipping over her face.

Mayor Strong stood on the side of the stage. He was smiling and holding a folded piece of paper in his hand.

Probably his speech, Nancy thought. *Mayor Strong loves making speeches.*

Nadine's hat fell off as she took a bow. Then the dancers tapped off the stage.

"Wasn't that great?" Mayor Strong asked as he walked onto the stage. He put on a pair of glasses, unfolded his speech, and began to read. "You know, when I was a kid—"

Nancy heard George groan under her breath. Mayor Strong always talked about being a kid.

"—we had only one ice-cream parlor, and it sold only two flavors!" Mayor Strong said. "Can you imagine that, kids?"

"Is he kidding?" a voice muttered. "I'd do a headstand on a pyramid for just *one* flavor."

Nancy turned around. Standing behind them was a boy from their class named Kevin Garcia.

Kevin's parents owned the Mean Bean Health Food Store on River Street. Kevin wasn't allowed to eat sweets, so he always mooched snacks from everybody's lunchboxes.

"What are you doing here, Kevin?" Nancy asked. "You're not allowed to eat ice cream."

"I heard Jim and Barry are giving away free samples of ice cream," Kevin said. He leaned closer to the girls and whispered, "Got any candy on you?"

"No," Nancy said.

"Hey," Kevin said. "Is it true that Kendra has a winning recipe for the contest?"

Bess and George raised their eyebrows at Nancy. She had told them that morning about Deirdre and her Web site.

"Um . . . maybe," Nancy blurted.

"Got any gum?" Kevin asked.

"No!" George said. "And don't ask us again!"

Kevin looked disappointed. He turned around and disappeared into the crowd.

"Kevin must have read Deirdre's Web site," Bess said.

Nancy looked for Kendra and found her in the crowd. Everyone near Kendra was pointing at her.

"I guess a *lot* of kids read Deirdre's Web site," Nancy said.

The mayor was still giving his speech. "I even remember riding my shiny red bicycle all the way to the next town for another flavor. But when I got there, they also had only two flavors!"

One or two people in the audience laughed.

"Where are Jim and Barry?" George asked. She stood on her tiptoes to see over the crowd. "I don't see them yet!"

"They're probably scooping out the free samples," Nancy said, rubbing her tummy.

"I hope it's not Marshmallow Martian," Bess said. She stuck her finger in her mouth, pretending to gag.

"Yes, Bess," Nancy said with a smile. "We know how much you hate green ice cream, no matter how good it is!"

A voice snapped, "What's wrong with Marshmallow Martian?"

Nancy, Bess, and George spun around. Standing behind them this time was fourth grader Daisy Dorfer and members of the Jim and Barry Fan Club. Daisy started the club for the summer. They met every week to taste a new Jim and Barry flavor that they picked out at the supermarket.

"Nothing's wrong with it," Bess said with a shrug. "It just makes me—"

"—want more!" Nancy cut in.

"Good," Daisy said. "Because Marshmallow Martian is my favorite flavor!"

Nancy heard Bess gagging under her breath.

"Um," Nancy said, trying to switch the subject. "Are you guys entering the contest?"

Peter Patino from the girls' third-grade class said, "Daisy's dad bought her an electronic ice-cream maker. It has digital controls and everything!"

"Now all we need is a recipe," fourth grader Melissa Rios said. She was wearing dangly ice-cream cone earrings.

Daisy planted her hands on her hips. "We'll

have one, okay?" she said. "And when we do-it'll be the best!"

"The best! The best!" the members chanted.

"It better be the best," Melissa whispered to Nancy. "Because we want to win more than anything!"

A roaring cheer made everyone face the stage.

"It's them!" Daisy swooned. "Jim and Barry!"

Jim and Barry waved to the crowd as they ran onto the stage. Nancy knew it was them from their picture on the ice-cream containers. Jim had copper red hair and wore round wire-rimmed glasses. Barry had a beard and wore a straw hat with a bright purple hatband.

"I scream, you scream, we all scream for ice cream!" Barry shouted.

"How do you like our new factory?" Jim called out. "Pretty cool, huh?"

Cheers filled the air.

"Who here thinks they can make an ice cream that'll rock our worlds?" Barry asked.

Nancy's hand shot up. So did dozens of others.

Jim held up a clipboard. "Well, then step right

up and put your names on the sign-up list!" he boomed.

The crowd began to squeeze into a single line. Deirdre Shannon ran over to Nancy, Bess, and George. She held up a camera and said, "Say Strawberry Cheesecake Ice Cream!"

"How about just cheese?" George asked.

"Cheese!" the three friends said as Deirdre snapped a picture. They knew the picture she was taking was for her Web site.

"Thanks," Deirdre said. "Now I've got to get a picture of Jim and Barry!"

Nancy glanced back. Kendra was lining up too. Daisy was standing right behind her, trying not to be bumped by Kendra's backpack.

I'm sure Kendra's recipe is still a secret, Nancy thought. *How could anyone steal it if it's inside her head?*

Nancy was about to inch her way up the line when she heard a voice yell, "Jim and Barry's flavors stink on ice!"

The girls turned their heads. Standing next to the line was Henderson, the son of Mr. Drippy.

He was holding a sign that read, JIM AND BARRY'S ICE CREAM MAKES ME BARF!

"Jim and Barry's ice cream gave me cooties!" Henderson shouted. "The raisins in the Rum Raisin are really ants! The cherries in the Cherry Vanilla are really squishy eyeballs. Alien eyeballs!"

"That's gross!" Bess said.

"So is Jim and Barry's ice cream!" Henderson said. He cackled meanly. Then he walked away

yelling, "Jim and Barry mix their ice cream with their feet!"

"That's one kid who won't be entering this contest," Nancy said. "He hates Jim and Barry's ice cream!"

The girls finally reached the sign-up list. They wrote their names neatly and clearly.

"We did it!" Bess said, jumping up and down.

"Now all we have to do is bring our Clueberry ice cream to the contest on Saturday!" Nancy said excitedly.

Next the girls picked up their free samples of Rootin' Tootin' Raspberry ice cream. They waited for Hannah as they ate out of little cups with tiny spoons.

"This flavor rocks!" George said.

"And it's not green." Bess sighed with relief.

Nancy was about to take another spoonful when Kendra ran over. Her dark eyes were flashing wildly.

"My s-secret r-r-recipe!" Kendra stammered. "Someone stole it!"

CHAPTER FOUR

Supermarket Surprise!

"How could it be stolen, Kendra?" Nancy asked. "The recipe was inside your head!"

"I wrote it on a piece of paper and brought it today," Kendra explained. "I wanted Jim and Barry to autograph it!"

Kendra held up her backpack. She pointed to the back pocket and said, "It was in that pocket. Now it's gone."

Deirdre ran over with her camera. "Hi, Kendra," she said. "Do you want to pose for my camera?"

Kendra stuck out her tongue and said, "How's that?"

"Not cool." Deirdre shook her head.

"Neither was telling the world I had a winning

recipe," Kendra said. "Now my recipe is stolen and I can't enter the contest!"

"Stolen?" Deirdre gasped. "No way!"

"You can still enter the contest, Kendra," George said. "You do know your recipe by heart, don't you?"

"Big deal," Kendra asked. "The thief who stole my recipe will probably make the same ice cream!"

"What are you going to do?" Bess asked.

"We have to find the robber by Saturday," Kendra said. "*Before* he or she enters the contest."

"We?" Nancy repeated.

"You *are* the Clue Crew, right?" Kendra asked.

"Right," George said. "But Saturday is in two days!"

Nancy felt sorry for Kendra. And she didn't want Kendra and Deirdre to fight. "We'll do it, Kendra," she said. "We'll help you find that creepy recipe thief."

Kendra heaved a sigh of relief. "Thanks, you guys!" she said.

Deirdre pointed her camera at Nancy, Bess, and George. "Smile and say, 'The Clue Crew is on the case!'" she said.

The girls each gave a thumbs-up as Deirdre took the picture.

"Perfect!" Deirdre said as she ran off.

Hannah honked her car horn as she drove up to the curb. Nancy, Bess, and George waved good-bye to Kendra as they climbed into the car.

"I know you can do it," Kendra called as the car pulled away. "The Clue Crew rules!"

When they reached the Drew house, the girls thundered up the stairs to their detective headquarters. Bess sat on Nancy's bed and bounced a stuffed unicorn on her lap. George sat at Nancy's desk and turned on the computer. Her eyes were glued to the screen as she began a new case file.

"If this mystery is about ice cream," Bess said, "does that make it a cold case?"

"No, Bess," Nancy said. "A cold case is a case that hasn't been solved. My dad told me that while we were watching a mystery show on TV."

"And we *are* going to solve this mystery," George said. "File's up. What do we know so far?"

Nancy paced across her shaggy lavender carpet. "The person who stole Kendra's recipe is probably a kid," she said slowly. "Someone who knew about the recipe and wants to win really badly."

"The Jim and Barry Fan Club wants to win badly," Bess said. "They said so themselves."

"And Daisy Dorfer was standing right behind Kendra in the sign-up line!" Nancy remembered.

"Daisy Dorfer," George said as she typed. "Suspect number one."

Bess tossed the unicorn in the air. "Kevin Garcia asked about Kendra's recipe," she said. "What about him?"

Nancy shook her head. "Why would Kevin enter a contest for something he can't eat?" she asked.

"Especially since his parents would have to sign a permission slip if he won," George added.

Next the girls thought of all the things the thief would need to make Kendra's recipe. First up: chocolate. Lots and lots of chocolate!

"Speaking of ice cream," George said. She

turned around in her chair. "I wonder how our flavor is doing."

"Let's taste it!" Bess said.

"We already tasted it," Nancy said.

George shrugged. "We didn't taste it after it was in the freezer for hours!" she said.

The girls raced out of Nancy's room and ran downstairs into the kitchen. Nancy opened the freezer and pulled out the ice-cream container. As she pulled off the lid—

"Woof!"

Chip jumped up against Nancy. She dropped the whole container on the floor with a *thunk!*

"No!" Nancy cried. Vanilla ice cream and blue-berries had spilled onto the floor in big frozen clumps.

The girls stared at Chip lapping up the ice cream.

"At least it wasn't chocolate." George sighed. "Chocolate isn't good for dogs."

Nancy felt awful. If only she had held the container tighter. If only she wasn't such a klutz!

“Now we’ll have to make our ice cream all over again,” Nancy said. “And that means buying more ingredients.”

Hannah came into the kitchen with a mop. “I’d drive you to the supermarket, girls,” she said. “But I have a casserole in the oven.”

"I'll call my mom," George said. "She goes to the supermarket almost every day."

Louise Fayne owned her own catering company. She planned parties all over River Heights and even provided the food. To Nancy, Mrs. Fayne's van always smelled like coleslaw and pickled tomatoes.

"I'm picking up fruit platters for Mayor Strong's birthday party this Saturday," Mrs. Fayne said as she drove her van. "It's going to be the party of the year!"

Nancy, Bess, and George sat behind Mrs. Fayne. The seat behind them was filled with coleslaw containers.

"Why is Mayor Strong's birthday party the same day as the ice-cream contest?" Bess asked.

"That's how it worked out," Mrs. Fayne said as she pulled the van into the supermarket parking lot.

Once inside the supermarket, Nancy saw lots of other kids. Their baskets and shopping carts were filled with all kinds of foods to make ice cream with.

"I have to go to the deli section," Mrs. Fayne said. "You can pick up your own items as long as you stay together and don't run."

The girls nodded. Shopping on their own always made them feel grown-up!

Mrs. Fayne walked away. Nancy grabbed a red plastic shopping basket, while George unfolded their shopping list. Bess walked to the dairy section for a container of milk. After putting it in the basket, they looked for blueberries.

"Fruit is against the wall," George said. "The healthy stuff is always against the walls."

Bess started to run down the aisle. "Last one there is a rotten watermelon!" she called.

"Bess, wait!" Nancy called. "We're not supposed to run in the supermarket, remember?"

Nancy and George raced after Bess. When they all reached the end of the aisle they sped around the corner.

Wham! The girls slammed right into Kevin Garcia!

Nancy dropped her basket with the container of milk. Luckily the milk didn't open and spill.

But everything tumbled out of Kevin's basket. There was a box of chocolate ice-cream pops, a package of chocolate-dipped ice-cream cones, two cans of chocolate drink, and three jumbo chocolate bars. Nancy stared at Kevin's packages on the floor. Kevin wasn't allowed to eat sweets. What was he doing with all that chocolaty stuff?

"Sorry, you guys," Bess said.

Kevin muttered something under his breath. He picked up his packages and shoved them back into his basket. Then he stood up and quickly walked away.

"Did you see that?" George asked.

"I sure did," Nancy said, nodding. "Kevin's basket was *chock full of chocolate*!"

CHAPTER FIVE

Sticks and Cones

"Kevin would need chocolate to make Kendra's ice-cream flavor," Bess said. "I told you he was a suspect!"

Nancy shook her head. "Kevin is always trying to get his hands on sweets," she said.

Tweeeeeee!!

The shrill sound of a whistle made the girls jump. Nancy whirled around. Daisy and the Jim and Barry Fan Club were standing at the end of the aisle. Daisy was wearing a yellow Jim and Barry Gorilla Vanilla T-shirt and a silver whistle around her neck.

"Okay, group!" Daisy said. "We have our shopping lists. Now let's move out!"

The fan club nodded. Then they spread out in many different directions.

"Daisy is one of our suspects," Nancy whispered. "Let's see what we can find out."

Daisy was wiping her whistle on her T-shirt when the girls walked over.

"Hi, Daisy," Nancy said. "Did you come up with a flavor for the contest?"

"You bet!" Daisy said. "And it's a sure winner!"

"What is it?" Bess asked.

"As if I'm going to tell you," Daisy said. "Only club members can know the top secret recipe."

Daisy swung her whistle as she walked away.

"Only members can know the top secret recipe," George mimicked. "Give me a break!"

"Let's follow the members around," Nancy said in a low voice. "And see what they're buying."

They were about to walk when—

"Girls!" Mrs. Fayne called. "We have to go now."

Nancy grabbed a carton of blueberries on their way to the checkout counter. They couldn't follow Daisy or the club. But they had a great clue. The fan club had a recipe. And it was top secret—just like Kendra's was!

"Now if we can just find out what it is!" Nancy said.

"Is your arm getting tired, George?" Nancy asked. George rolled the coffee can back and forth over the Faynes' doorstep.

"Nah, I'm on a roll!" George joked.

The girls were in the Faynes' front yard making their second batch of ice cream. They didn't want to be near Chip when their ice cream was finished.

"Can I taste it now?" Bess asked. She waved a plastic spoon in the air.

"Don't start that again, Bess," George groaned.

"Hey, Clue Crew!" a voice called.

The girls looked up. Their friend Marcy Rubin was passing by the yard with her five-year-old sister, Cassidy.

"Hi-yeee!" Cassidy called. "Want to see my brand-new sneakers?"

"They're not new, Cassidy," Marcy said. "They used to belong to me."

Cassidy stared down at her red and white sneakers. "No wonder they smell," she said.

Nancy, Bess, and George walked over to Marcy.

"We were just making ice cream for the contest, Marcy," Nancy said.

"How do you have time?" Marcy asked. "Aren't you guys solving the case of Kendra's missing ice-cream recipe?"

Nancy, Bess, and George shared surprised looks.

"Who told you that?" Nancy asked.

"I read it on Deirdre's Web site," Marcy said. "She wrote that the Clue Crew will solve the case for sure. There was even a neat picture of you guys all giving a thumbs-up!"

"Did she give away Kendra's recipe?" Nancy asked.

"Nope," Marcy said.

Nancy sighed with relief. "At least she didn't do that," she said.

"Hey," Marcy said, looking to her side. "Where's Cassidy?"

The girls spun around. Cassidy was sitting on the doorstep eating Clue-berry ice cream from the coffee can!

"Yummy for the tummy!" Cassidy shouted.

"Drop that spoon now, you little pest!" Marcy shouted as she raced over to Cassidy.

"Our second batch of ice cream," George groaned.

"Maybe we aren't meant to enter this contest." Bess sighed.

Nancy smiled as she watched Marcy wrestling the spoon out of her little sister's hand.

"Oh, yes we are," Nancy said. "Cassidy likes it. So maybe Jim and Barry will too!"

"I think Daisy did it, Dad," Nancy said that night. "She was standing right behind Kendra. And she said their new recipe was top secret and a winner!"

Mr. Drew looked up from the newspaper he was reading. He liked reading the paper in his favorite chair every night. "Try not to jump to conclusions, Nancy," he said.

Nancy wrinkled her nose and said, "Jump where?"

"It means don't end your case before you check out everything," Mr. Drew said with a smile. "Things aren't always what they seem to be, you know."

"Okay, Daddy," Nancy said. "But it sure seems like Daisy took Kendra's recipe."

It was still light outside, so Nancy had permission to play in the yard. With Chip at her heels, she skipped to the front door.

"Come on, Chip," Nancy said. "Let's see if you can catch a Frisbee!"

Nancy swung the front door open. As she stepped outside she felt something crunch under her foot. She looked down and gasped. A message had been left on her doorstep. It read, "GIVE UP!"

Nancy looked closer.

The message was written with wooden Popsicle sticks!

Chapter Six

Club Flub

"Eww, don't touch them!" Bess warned. "If they're Popsicle sticks—they've been licked!"

It was Friday morning. The Popsicle sticks from the weird message the night before were spread out on Nancy's desk.

"Licked Popsicle sticks usually have ice-cream stains on them," Nancy said. "These don't."

"That makes it even weirder!" George said.

Nancy picked up a stick and flipped it over in her hand. "Each stick has the words Lickety Sticks Company stamped on it," she said. "That must be the place where these Popsicle sticks were made."

"Who would leave such a creepy message?" Bess asked.

"Thanks to Deirdre, everyone knows we're trying to solve Kendra's case," Nancy said. "So the person who stole Kendra's recipe probably wants us to give up."

"But who would have that many Popsicle sticks?" Bess asked.

The girls thought in silence. Suddenly George snapped her fingers and said, "Kevin had a box of Popsicles in his shopping basket."

"A box like that holds only six Popsicles," Nancy said. "A lot more sticks were used to write that message."

"Maybe it's more than one person," Bess said. "Daisy's fan club eats ice cream all the time. And Jim and Barry make Popsicles too."

"I wish we could go to a club meeting," Nancy said. "Then we could find out what kind of ice cream they're making for the contest."

George pointed to a calendar hanging over Nancy's desk. "Today is Friday," she said. "Doesn't the Jim and Barry Fan Club meet every Friday?"

"How can we go to go a meeting if we're not members?" Bess asked.

The girls didn't say a word as they thought. Then Nancy had a brainstorm.

"I know! Let's join the club!" Nancy said.

"I don't want to join that dumb club!" Bess whined. "Daisy is so bossy."

"And we already have a club," George said. "A detective club."

"We'll just be joining to get their top secret recipe," Nancy explained. "We don't have to go to any meetings after that."

The girls knew that Daisy lived on Sparrow Street. George turned on the computer and found Daisy's street on a special Map Search site.

"Only four blocks away," George announced. "We can go there together."

Bess and George already had their bikes and helmets at Nancy's house. Nancy grabbed hers and the three pedaled to Daisy's house.

As the girls rode, the Mr. Drippy truck rambled past them. Henderson stuck his head out the window and shouted, "Ewww! It's the Clue Creeeeew!"

"How does he know we're the Clue Crew?" Bess called from her bike.

"Probably from school," Nancy called back.

"We're famous!" George declared with a smile.

The three girls turned onto Sparrow Street. They parked their bikes against a big tree on the sidewalk. Then they walked up the cobblestone path to Daisy's house.

A teenage boy opened the door after the girls knocked. "You're here for my sister's meeting?" he asked. "So what's the secret password?"

Password? The girls traded worried looks.

"Um . . . cone?" Nancy guessed.

"Sprinkles?" Bess asked.

"Banana split?" George said.

The boy stared at the girls. Then he cracked up laughing. "There is no password!" he said. "You fell for it. I am so gooooood!"

George rolled her eyes as the boy yelled for his sister. "Brothers!" she groaned. "I've got two of them!"

Daisy came running to the door. She looked surprised to see Nancy, Bess, and George.

"Hi, Daisy," Nancy said. "We want to join the Jim and Barry Fan Club!"

"You want to join right before the contest?" Daisy asked. "You don't want to steal our secret recipe, do you?"

"No way!" Nancy said. "We have our own recipe for the contest, remember?"

Daisy folded her arms as she looked from Nancy to Bess to George. "Okay," she said. "But every member has to pass a taste test first."

"You mean taste ice cream?" Bess asked.

"All right!" George cheered. "That's one pop quiz we *want* to take!"

Nancy, Bess, and George followed Daisy into the house. As they walked through the kitchen, Daisy introduced them to her mother. Mrs. Dorfer was on her knees stuffing cans and boxes into a big blue recycling bag. Daisy then led the girls downstairs to the basement. The fan club was sitting cross-legged on the floor. Melissa and Peter waved to the girls. Nancy thought most of the kids looked friendly.

"Peter's T-shirt says Marshmallow Martian," Bess whispered. "Yuck-o!"

"Shhh!" Nancy warned. "We have to love all the flavors or they won't let us join the club."

Daisy walked to a desk near the door. She held up a writing pad and said, "I just wrote our recipe nice and neat for Jim and Barry to read tomorrow."

Nancy, Bess, and George stepped forward.

"Nuh-uh!" Daisy said. She ripped the page off the writing pad. "Not until you join the club."

"Sure," Nancy said. "Let the taste test begin!"

Soon Nancy, Bess, and George were sitting on chairs in the middle of the room. Club members giggled as they tied colorful bandannas over the girls' eyes. Nancy couldn't see but she could hear everyone chatting excitedly. She could even smell something sweet—like ice cream!

"George is first," Daisy said. "Give her the bowl, Melissa."

Nancy heard George's spoon clatter against ceramic. Then she heard a gulp as if George was swallowing.

"Well?" Daisy asked.

"It has a definite nutty taste," George's voice said. "With a touch of caramel . . . and just a hint of—"

"What is it already?" a boy demanded.

"Peanut Brittle Blast!" George said.

The club members applauded.

"Correct," Daisy said. "You can take your blindfold off, George."

Next was Nancy's turn. She felt an ice-cream bar being shoved into her hand. Taking a bite, she began to chew. The ice cream was crunchy, as if it had bits of candy inside.

"I'm pretty sure this is Toffee Coffee," Nancy said.

More applause.

"You guys are good!" Daisy exclaimed.

Nancy whipped off her blindfold. Still eating the ice cream, she turned to George and winked.

"Bess is last," Daisy said. "Give her the ice cream, Melissa."

Melissa smiled as she stepped forward with a bowl. Nancy gasped when she saw the mound of ice cream inside the bowl. It was bright green!

Oh, no! Nancy thought. *It's Marshmallow Martian!*

Chapter Seven

Candy-Handed

Nancy glanced sideways at George. She was staring at the green ice cream too.

"Um, Daisy," Nancy said. "That flavor is too easy!"

"What are you talking about?" Daisy asked.

"Bess likes hard test questions!" George piped in.

"Since when?" Bess said. She smiled under her blindfold and shouted, "Bring it on!"

Nancy held her breath as Bess took the bowl. Still blindfolded, Bess felt around for the spoon. Carefully she took a spoonful, than stuck it straight into her mouth.

Bess's chin moved up and down. Suddenly her eyebrows flew up above the blindfold. She puffed out her cheeks and spit the ice cream back into the bowl. "Bleeeech!! Marshmallow Martian! Gross! Phooey!"

Bess whipped off her blindfold. She jumped up, leaving the bowl of ice cream on her chair. Nancy and George jumped up too.

"Maybe there was a hair in it!" Nancy said.

The club members stared open-mouthed at Bess. Daisy folded her arms across her chest and said, "We only take members who love *all* of Jim and Barry's ice-cream flavors."

"Yeah," Peter sneered. "Maybe Mr. Drippy has a fan club you can join!"

Nancy stared back at the club members. They didn't look so friendly anymore.

"Er—we have to go," Nancy said quickly.

"We have tons of homework!" George said.

"In July?" Daisy asked.

"It's never too early to start!" Nancy said with a smile. In a flash the girls raced out of the basement room. They said a polite good-bye to Mrs. Dorfer, then raced out of the house to their bikes.

"It's my fault!" Bess wailed. "I blew it!"

Nancy took one last bite of her ice-cream bar. "You were just being honest, Bess," she said. "Besides, we didn't want to join that club anyway."

"Now we'll never find out their secret recipe for the contest," Bess wailed.

"Who says we won't?" George asked.

Nancy and Bess turned to George. She was holding a piece of paper in her hand and grinning from ear to ear.

"Look what I grabbed on the way out," George said. "It's the paper that was underneath the recipe they wrote."

"It's blank!" Bess said.

"Not exactly," George said. She pointed to the

paper. "Check out the scratches on it. Those are the marks the pen made when Daisy wrote the recipe on the top page."

"I get it!" Nancy said. "If we can read the scratches, we can read the recipe."

"How?" Bess asked.

Nancy stuck the Popsicle stick in her pocket. She pulled a pencil out of her waist pack and said, "Watch. It's a trick I learned in a mystery book."

Nancy used the side of the pencil point to lightly draw over the scratches. The words appeared like magic!

"What does it say?" Bess asked.

The girls studied the paper.

"It says . . .

'Oatmeal Cookie and Raisin Crunch Ice Cream,'" Nancy said. "Not Chock Full of Chocolate."

"How do we know it's for real?" George asked. "Maybe they just wrote a fake recipe to trick us."

Nancy carried the Popsicle stick to a trash can in front of the Dorfers' house. On the side-walk next to the can was a big blue recycling bag—the same bag Mrs. Dorfer was stuffing things into before.

Nancy kneeled down and peered through the clear blue plastic. "Look!" she said, pointing with the Popsicle stick. "This bag is filled with empty raisin containers and oatmeal cookie boxes."

George looked at the list of ingredients on the scratchy paper. "That's what they used to make the ice cream," she said. "I guess the club didn't make Chock Full of Chocolate."

Nancy glanced at the Jim and Barry Popsicle stick in her hand. The words "Lickety Sticks Com-pany" were not stamped on it. "They didn't write the creepy message, either," she said.

The girls took the Jim and Barry Fan Club off

the suspect list. They decided to sit down and come up with more suspects.

"Can we talk over fruit smoothies?" George asked.

"But we just had ice cream!" Nancy said.

"I only had one spoonful," George said.

"And I spit mine out," Bess said. "So that doesn't count."

The girls pedaled their bikes two blocks to River Street. As they parked them, they noticed a sign in the window of the Mean Bean Health Food Store. It read SMOOTHIES! 100% REAL FRUIT.

Nancy, Bess, and George walked inside. The store always smelled like the inside of a vitamin bottle.

"This is the place that Kevin's parents own," George whispered. "If he's here, maybe we can ask him questions."

"Sure," Nancy said. But deep inside she still didn't think Kevin stole Kendra's recipe.

Mr. Garcia stood behind the juice counter. He made three smoothies—strawberry for Bess, banana for George, and banana-strawberry for Nancy.

"Is Kevin here?" Bess asked.

Mrs. Garcia walked over from the vitamin shelf. "Kevin is out spending his birthday money," she said.

"Hopefully on that new Yoga for Kids DVD!" Mr. Garcia said with a grin. "I heard it really rocks!"

"Can we add some wheat grass juice to your smoothies?" Mrs. Garcia asked. "Very healthy!"

"And tasty!" Mr. Garcia added.

"Grass?" George gulped.

"Um . . . no, thank you," Nancy said.

The three friends carried their smoothies out of the store. They were about to stick their straws through the plastic lids when Kendra huffed over.

"Smoothies?" Kendra cried. "You're supposed to be finding out who stole my recipe. The contest is tomorrow!"

"We were having a high-energy snack," George

said. "So we'll have lots of strength to solve the case!"

But Nancy knew Kendra was right. Time was running out.

"We'll do our best, Kendra," Nancy promised.

Kendra heaved a big sigh. Then she ran to catch up with her mother.

"We *have* to solve this case, Clue Crew," Nancy said. "Let's sit down somewhere and really get to work!"

The girls saw a bench in front of the Chocolate Soldier Shop. As they walked toward it, the door of the shop swung open. A boy rushed out with a box tucked under his arm. On the box was a picture of a chocolate soldier.

"It's Kevin," Nancy whispered.

The girls ducked behind the bench. Between the wooden slats they watched Kevin running to a shiny blue bike parked at the curb. He dropped the box into the bike basket, then pulled on a helmet, climbed on, and pedaled away.

"That didn't look like a yoga DVD to me,"

George said. "He spent his birthday money on chocolate!"

"No one can eat that much chocolate," Bess asked. "Not even Kevin Garcia!"

"Unless he's not eating it," Nancy said slowly.

"What do you mean?" George asked.

"Maybe Kevin *did* enter the ice-cream contest," Nancy said slowly. "And maybe he *is* making Kendra's ice cream!"

CHAPTER EIGHT

Ice Scream!

"Let's follow Kevin on our bikes," Nancy suggested. "And see what he's up to."

"And lose our awesome fruit smoothies?" George asked. "Nuh-uh!"

The girls sat on the bench slurping their drinks.

"Maybe there's a way to find out if Kevin entered the ice-cream contest," Nancy said.

"The Jim and Barry Ice Cream Factory is on this street," George said. "Do you think the guys would let us see the sign-up list?"

"We can ask them," Nancy said.

The girls finished their smoothies. Then they rode their bikes all the way down the street to the Jim and Barry Ice Cream Factory. After filing through the revolving doors they looked around. The lobby wall was covered with pictures of Jim and Barry. A guard was sitting at a big wooden desk. Her nameplate read BEVERLY SHAW.

"We're not giving away ice cream, kids," Beverly said.

"We don't want any ice cream," Nancy said.

"We just want to see the sign-up list for the contest, please," George said.

"Sorry, girls," Beverly said. "That list is private."

"Then can we meet Jim and Barry?" Bess asked.

"Jim and Barry are hard at work," Beverly said, shaking her head. "They're coming up with the next flavor."

"What is it?" Nancy asked.

"That's private too," Beverly said. Her phone rang. She picked it up and said, "Jim and Barry's Ice Cream."

The girls traded glances as Beverly began talking. There had to be a way to get inside the factory and speak to Jim and Barry!

"Hold on, sir. I'll check the calendar," Beverly

said into the phone. She opened her desk drawer and began rummaging through it.

"Come on!" George hissed.

In a blink, the girls were tiptoeing quickly and quietly down the hallway. At the end of the hall was a big steel door. A sign on it read EMPLOYEES ONLY!

"What are em-ploy-ees?" Nancy asked.

"Maybe kids who signed up for the ice-cream contest!" George said with a smile. "Are we lucky or what?"

The girls pushed at the door until it swung open.

"Brr!" Bess said as they walked into the room. "It's freezing in here!"

The room was brightly lit and sparkling clean. It was filled with big steel vats. The vats were almost as tall as the girls.

"No wonder it's cold," Nancy said, rubbing her arms. "This must be where they make the ice cream!"

George ran over to a vat. She grabbed the rim and hoisted herself up. Then she peered into the vat and said, "Wowie! I think this is my favorite—Whoooaaaaaa!"

Nancy gasped. George was falling headfirst into the vat! She and Bess grabbed George's feet and held on tight.

"I like ice cream, but not this much!" George shouted. "Heeeelp!"

"We're trying!" Nancy grunted. She and Bess tugged on George's feet until they finally pulled her out of the vat.

"Whew!" George said. "That was close!"

"No," a voice said. "That was Mint, Mint, Hooray!"

The girls whirled around. Jim and Barry were standing in the room.

Nancy stared at the guys. They wore white coats and hairnets over their hair.

"We're not giving tours yet, kids," Jim said.

"The door said . . . em-ploy-ees," George said. "That means—"

"People who work here," Barry explained with a grin. "You're a bit young for a factory job."

"And you shouldn't be here without a grown-up," Jim added.

"Sorry," Nancy said. "We just wanted to see the sign-up list for the ice-cream contest tomorrow."

"We're already on the list," George said. "But we want to see if someone from school is on it too."

"Can we?" Bess asked. "Please?"

"No can do," Jim said.

"But we can't wait to taste your ice cream tomorrow," Barry said brightly. "Just try not to fall into it!"

The guys held the door for Nancy, Bess, and George as they left the big, cold room.

"How neat was that?" Bess squealed. "We got to meet Jim and Barry—up close and personal!"

"But we didn't get to see the list." Nancy sighed. "And when the guard sees that we sneaked in—she's going to have kittens!"

As they neared the guard's desk, Nancy noticed something. There was a *different* guard at the desk this time. His nameplate read MATT STEVENSON.

"Brainstorm," George whispered.

Nancy and Bess followed George to the desk.

"Hi," George said. "We just want to make sure our names are spelled right on the contest list."

Matt reached into the top drawer of his desk and pulled out the sign-up sheet. "Here you go!" he said.

The girls huddled over the list. Bess jabbed her finger at one of the names: Kevin Garcia!

"Did you spell your names right?" Matt asked.

"Yes!" the girls said together.

"Then good luck in the contest tomorrow,"

Matt said. "And if you win, save a pint of ice cream for me!"

Nancy, Bess, and George zipped through the revolving doors. Once outside, they raced toward their bikes.

"Kevin *did* enter the contest," George said.

"We have to check Kevin out," Nancy said. "But I have no idea where he lives."

"Me neither," George said with a shrug.

"Two hundred Crescent Street!" Bess said. "It was right next to his name."

"How do you know?" Nancy asked.

"Not only can I build and fix things," Bess said proudly, "I have a great memory too!"

The girls pedaled the three blocks to Crescent Street. They found Kevin's house in the middle of the block. They stepped up to the door, and Nancy rang the doorbell over and over again. They walked to a window and peeked inside. The Garcias' housekeeper was busy vacuuming the living room.

Rrrrr! Rrrrr!

"No wonder she can't hear the doorbell,"

George said. "That vacuum cleaner sounds like a rocket booster!"

Nancy saw a path leading around the house to the backyard. "Let's check out the back," she said. "Kevin might be hanging out there."

"Or making ice cream!" Bess said with a frown.

The girls followed the path to the backyard. They didn't see Kevin, just some patio furniture and a small white toolshed.

Suddenly Nancy spotted something on the grass near the shed. It looked like a crumpled-up candy bar wrapper. She picked it up and flattened it out. It was a wrapper from the Chocolate Soldier Shop.

"That's where Kevin bought the chocolate," Nancy said.

"Maybe Kevin made the ice cream already," George said. "And he's stashing it in a freezer inside the shed."

Nancy wanted to look inside. She turned the handle on the shed door. The wooden door creaked as she pushed it open.

The girls filed inside the shed. They jumped as the door slammed shut. With only one tiny window, it was very dark in the shed!

"Let's go," George said. "I don't see any—"

"Oooooh!" a voice moaned.

Nancy froze.

"Oooooh!"

There it was again! Nancy felt Bess grab her arm.

"Wh-what was th-that?" Bess stammered. "A ghost?"

CHAPTER NINE

What's for Dessert?

"Ooooh—my stomach!" the voice moaned.

"That's not a ghost," Nancy said. "It's Kevin!"

George opened the door for light. Behind a pile of firewood the girls found Kevin. He was sitting on the floor, surrounded by crumpled candy bar wrappers, a chocolate drink can, and an empty Popsicle box!

"Aha!" George said. "Caught chocolate-handed!"

"What are you doing here?" Kevin groaned. His face was smudged with chocolate stains. So was his white T-shirt.

"We're looking for Chock Full of Chocolate ice cream," Bess said with a smirk. "Got any?"

"Chocolate!" Kevin groaned. He stuck out his

tongue and made a gagging sound. "Don't even say the word!"

Nancy felt bad that Kevin had a stomachache. But she was aching to ask him questions!

"What's the deal with all this chocolate,

Kevin?" Nancy asked. "You're not even allowed to eat it."

"That's why I spent my birthday money on tons of the stuff," Kevin explained. "My mom and dad said I could spend it on anything I wanted."

"So you ate it *all*?" Bess asked.

"Yeah. But don't remind me!" Kevin groaned again.

"Your name was on the contest list," George said. "Weren't you going to use the chocolate to make ice cream?"

"Some of it," Kevin admitted. "But I kept eating and eating and eating until nothing was left."

"I don't get it, Kevin," Nancy said. "Why did you enter a contest to win something you can't eat?"

"That's the idea!" Kevin said. "If I had that silver ticket, I'd be able to eat all the ice cream I wanted."

"Not if your parents have to sign a permission slip, too," Nancy pointed out.

Kevin stared at Nancy. Then he slapped his forehead with the back of his hand. "A permission slip?" he said. "Now you tell me!"

Nancy saw a Popsicle stick on the floor. As she kneeled down to pick it up, Kevin burped. His eyes bulged out as he covered his mouth with his hand.

"Back up! He's going to hurl!" George shouted.

The girls raced out of the shed. They were halfway through the yard when Nancy decided to run back.

"Kevin?" Nancy called through the door. "Are you okay?"

"Yeah," Kevin called back. "Just a dry heave."

Nancy, Bess, and George walked slowly back to their bikes.

"I guess Kevin is innocent," Bess said.

Nancy examined the Popsicle stick she took from the shed. "This doesn't say 'Lickety Sticks' on it," she said. "So Kevin did not write the message on my doorstep."

"Now we really have zero suspects." George sighed. "And the contest is tomorrow!"

Nancy suddenly heard bells. The Mr. Drippy truck was rolling down the street. It pulled up to the sidewalk and stopped.

The girls watched as a six-year-old boy made his way to the truck. He seemed to know the drill as he approached the window and saluted Mr. Drippy. "One vanilla ice-cream bar, please!" he said.

"At ease, young man," Mr. Drippy said.

While Mr. Drippy dug through the freezer, Nancy looked through the truck window. Henderson was standing in the back of the truck. He had two Popsicle sticks stuck up his nose and was snorting like a walrus!

"Gross!" Bess muttered.

Nancy was about to turn away from Henderson when something clicked. She ran over to the boy with the ice-cream bar and said, "Can we see that pop?" she asked.

"Sorry," the boy said. "You forgot to say—"

"Please!" Nancy groaned.

The boy looked confused as Nancy examined the Popsicle stick. "Bingo!" Nancy said. "This stick has 'Lickety Sticks Company' stamped on it!"

Nancy gave the ice-cream bar back to the boy. He walked away, shaking his head.

"Maybe Henderson wrote the Popsicle stick message, Nancy!" Bess said.

"Why would Henderson tell us to give up?" George asked. "He didn't enter the contest."

Nancy shrugged. "Maybe Henderson read about our case on Deirdre's Web site," she said. "And was just being pesty."

"Like always." Bess sighed.

It was two o'clock in the afternoon. George had promised to watch her baby brother while her mother planned the mayor's party. Bess's grandparents were visiting that afternoon, so she wanted to go home.

"That's okay," Nancy said with a smile. "I'll work on the case alone for a while."

Nancy knew it wouldn't be easy. Especially when the contest was tomorrow and she didn't have a clue.

"I don't know what to do, Daddy," Nancy said that evening. "Kendra wanted us to find the ice-cream thief in time for the contest tomorrow. And we blew it!"

Mr. Drew was busy chopping carrots for the dinner salad. "No, you didn't," he said. "Clues can show up anytime—even at the last minute."

Nancy smiled as her dad popped a carrot slice into her mouth. She swallowed and said, "I sure hope so, Daddy. Because this *is* the last minute!"

"Hi, George," Nancy said. "Are you ready for the contest?"

It was Saturday morning. Nancy and Bess

were standing on the Faynes' doorstep. In less than an hour the Jim and Barry Ice-Cream Flavor Contest would begin.

George waved Nancy and Bess inside. "I guess," she said. "But I'm bummed out about not solving the case."

"You're not the only one." Nancy sighed.

What would they tell Kendra when they saw her? And what would happen to the Clue Crew now? Would they be the big joke of River Heights Elementary School?

The girls walked into the kitchen. Mrs. Fayne was talking loudly on the phone.

"We didn't order orange carnations!" she said. "We ordered red roses! Red roses!"

"Mayor Strong's birthday party is today," George whispered. "My mom is so nervous she almost brushed her teeth with sunscreen this morning."

Nancy saw a big cardboard box on the kitchen table. "What are those?" she asked.

"Just the menus for the party," George said.

"Anything yummy on it?" Bess asked.

"If it's not a pizza party—who cares?" George said.

Bess picked up a menu and began to read out loud: "They're having something called Caesar Salad. The main course is salmon and asparagus. And for dessert there's . . . Chock Full of Chocolate Ice Cream."

Nancy blinked hard.

Say what?

"Bess!" she said. "Did you just say what I think you just said?"

Chapter Ten

Choco-Late!

"That's what it says," Bess said. "See for yourself!"

All three girls examined the menu.

"It *is* Chock Full of Chocolate Ice Cream!" Nancy said.

"*The* Chock Full of Chocolate Ice Cream?" George asked.

"It's got to be Kendra's recipe!" Nancy said. "But how did it land up on the menu for the mayor's party?"

"Mom!" George called. "How did you get Chock Full of Chocolate Ice Cream for the party?"

Mrs. Fayne was just hanging up the phone. "I didn't, George," she said. "Three gallons of it were delivered to Mayor Strong yesterday as a birthday present."

"By whom?" Nancy asked.

"I don't know," Mrs. Fayne said. "But I had to change the menu at the last minute."

The phone rang and Mrs. Fayne picked it up. "Hello?" she said. "No! I ordered *bagels*—not beagles!"

Nancy couldn't believe it. Her dad was right. Clues sometimes *did* pop up at the last minute!

"We have to go to the mayor's house," Nancy told Bess and George. "And find out who sent that ice cream."

Bess looked at her blue wristwatch. "But the ice-cream contest is in less than half an hour," she said. "We have to bring our Clue-berry ice cream to the factory!"

"We'll take it with us," Nancy said. "Come on!"

Bess grabbed the pint of Clue-berry from the Faynes' freezer. They rushed out of the house and ran the short distance to the mayor's house. On the way a voice yelled out, "Clue Crew! Wait up!"

Nancy glanced over her shoulder. It was Kendra, running right behind them!

"The ice-cream contest is today!" Kendra

shouted. "Did you solve the case? Well, did you?"

"We'll find out soon, Kendra!" Nancy shouted back.

The girls were out of breath when they reached the mayor's big yellow house. Nancy used the shiny brass knocker to rap on the door. The mayor himself answered the door. He smiled when he saw the girls.

"Happy birthday!" Nancy blurted. "Can you please tell us who gave you Chock Full of Chocolate ice cream?"

The mayor smiled. "Chock Full of Chocolate," he said. "You know, when I was a kid, chocolate was my favorite—"

"Please, Mayor Strong!" George cut in.

Mayor Strong's eyes widened. "All righty then," he said. "The ice cream was given to me by Chuck Murphy."

"Who's he?" Nancy asked.

"You kids know him as Mr. Drippy," Mayor Strong said. "Now I'd better get ready for my birthday party."

The girls stared at the door as it closed.

"Excuse me," Kendra said. "But how did that mean Mr. Drippy get my ice-cream recipe?"

As Nancy thought, she remembered Henderson.

"Henderson was at the factory on sign-up day," Nancy said. "Maybe he stole the recipe to give to his dad."

"Why would *he* steal my recipe?" Kendra asked.

A boy suddenly whizzed by on a skateboard. Nancy couldn't believe their luck. It was Henderson!

"Why don't we ask him?" Nancy said.

The four girls raced after Henderson.

"Henderson Drippy—I mean Murphy!" Nancy called. "We have to ask you something!"

Henderson looked back. He kicked and kicked to make his board go faster.

Nancy, Bess, George, and Kendra picked up speed. But they weren't quick enough for a speeding skateboard!

They were about to give up when another friend rattled down the block on roller skates. It was Deirdre Shannon!

Deirdre sped after Henderson. She caught

up to him and yelled, "Stoooooopppp!"

Henderson's board flipped out from under his feet. As he tried to catch it, Nancy, Bess, George, and Kendra raced over.

"I know what you want," Henderson said. "So I did write the message with the Popsicle sticks. Get over it!"

"We know you wrote the message," Nancy said. "But how did your dad get Chock Full of Chocolate ice cream?"

"What's the big deal?" Henderson asked. "I didn't want everyone buying Jim and Barry's ice cream instead of my dad's. So when I found this cool recipe for Chock Full of Chocolate, I gave it to him!"

"Did you say . . . found?" Kendra asked.

"Yeah," Henderson said. "It was on the ground."

Nancy turned slowly to Kendra. "Kendra," she said. "Your backpack doesn't have a hole in it . . . does it?"

Kendra took off her backpack. She touched the bottom of the front pocket and gulped. "Whoops," she said.

Nancy felt the slit under the pocket. It was wide enough for a small piece of paper to fall out.

"Sorry, you guys," Kendra said. She turned to Deirdre. "You're not going to write about this, will you?"

"Not if you don't want me to," Deirdre said.

"Chock Full of Chocolate is still your flavor, Kendra," Nancy said gently. "You can still enter the contest."

"The contest is in a few minutes," Kendra wailed. "I can't whip up a new batch of ice cream by then!"

"Oh, yeah?" Henderson said. "Watch this!"

Henderson put two fingers in his mouth and let out three sharp whistles. In a few seconds the Mr. Drippy truck rolled around the corner!

"Dad!" Henderson said as the truck stopped. "This is Kendra. She invented the Chock Full of Chocolate recipe."

The girls expected Mr. Drippy to glare at Kendra and insist that Chock Full of Chocolate was his recipe now. Instead Mr. Drippy smiled and said, "Good job, young lady!"

"Thanks," Kendra said. "But I don't have any to enter in the contest."

Mr. Drippy picked up a big cardboard box. On it was written "Chock Full of Chocolate." "Then you're going to need this!" he declared.

"My ice-cream flavor made into ice-cream pops!" Kendra exclaimed. "Cool!"

The girls raced around the corner to the Jim and Barry's Ice Cream Factory. Mr. Drippy's truck followed, his jingle blaring. At the factory, Nancy, Bess, George, and Kendra ran up onto the stage with their ice creams. Kendra smiled as she held a Chock Full of Chocolate ice-cream pop. Nancy was proud to hold their container of Clue-berry.

After another dance number by the tapping ice-cream cones, Jim and Barry stepped up to the microphone. They wore T-shirts with tuxedos printed on them.

"Let the contest begin!" Jim shouted.

Jim and Barry went down the line, tasting each flavor of ice cream. They liked the fan club's Oatmeal Raisin Cookie Crunch. They loved Kendra's Chock Full of Chocolate.

"It's our turn," Bess whispered as Jim and Barry walked over.

"And what's your ice cream called?" Jim asked.

"Clue-berry!" Nancy, Bess, and George said together.

"Snappy name," Barry said. "Let's have a taste."

Nancy smiled as she handed Barry the container. But when he pulled off the lid, the container tipped and—

Splat!

Nancy, Bess, and George gulped as they stared

at the puddle on the stage. Their Clue-berry ice cream had melted!

"Um," George said. "Can we enter a milk-shake?"

"Maybe next year," Jim said.

"But nice try, girls," Barry said.

As the guys walked to the next contestant, Nancy felt awful. But what did they expect after carrying their ice cream around in the hot sun for almost an hour?

In the end, the winner wasn't Kendra. Or the Jim and Barry Fan Club. To everyone's surprise, it was Kevin Garcia!

At the last minute Kevin came up with an entry called Naturally Nutty. It was made with frozen yogurt, dried apricots, and all kinds of nuts.

It was the perfect flavor for Jim and Barry. Especially since they wanted to sell a healthier new frozen dessert!

After the contest, Kevin waved his silver ticket in one hand. In the other hand was his parents' permission slip.

"My mom and dad said I can visit the factory once a month," Kevin explained. "So long as I pick a flavor they think is okay."

"What are you going to pick first?" Nancy asked.

"Anything but chocolate!" Kevin said, laughing.

Kendra ran over with a big smile. "Guess what?" she said. "Mr. Drippy is naming my ice cream after me. So every bar will say Kendra's Chock Full of Chocolate!"

"Way to go," Nancy cheered.

"You'll be as famous as Jim and Barry!" George said.

"I can't wait to write about this contest," Deirdre said. "Nancy, Bess, George? Can I call your ice cream Goo-berry?"

"*No*!" the three girls said together.

"Oh well." Deirdre sighed. "Come on, Kendra. Pose in front of the Mr. Drippy truck so I can take your picture."

Nancy was glad that Kendra and Deirdre were friends again. But she *was* sad that Clue-berry turned out to be a mushy mess. As they waited for Hannah to pick them up, Nancy, Bess, and George talked about the contest.

"We lost," Bess said sadly.

"Big-time!" George added.

Nancy turned to her two best friends and smiled.

"But we did solve the case, Clue Crew," she said. "And that makes us winning detectives!"

Nancy, Bess, and George's Coffee-Can Ice Cream

Nancy, Bess, and George know that making ice cream can be as easy as one, two, freeze! All you need is a sweet tooth and these simple ingredients:

1/2 cup milk
1/2 teaspoon vanilla
1 tablespoon sugar
4 cups crushed ice
4 tablespoons salt
Standard size coffee can with plastic lid
*Economy size (jumbo) coffee can with plastic lid.
A hand towel or gloves to keep fingers from freezing. Brr!

E-Z INSTRUCTIONS:

Mix the milk, vanilla, and sugar together in the smaller coffee can. Seal the can with the plastic lid. Put the can inside the larger can. Fill the larger can with ice and salt, and seal with the plastic lid. Now you have one can inside another!

READY TO ROLL!

Using your hand, roll the can back and forth on the ground until the ice cream is firm. Five to ten minutes is enough time for the mixture to freeze.

Now here comes the best part. . . . Grab a spoon, dig in, and enjoy!

FUN FACTOID

The ice-cream cone was invented at the St. Louis expo in 1904! The vendor ran out of plates and used rolled-up waffles instead! The rest is ice-cream history!

(*No jumbo coffee can at home? Try a restaurant or teacher's cafeteria for an empty one!)

A pony on the front lawn? Impossible!

Saturday morning after breakfast, Nancy was getting dressed when she heard a strange sound outside her window. Looking out, she saw the cutest, shaggiest little pony standing on her front lawn! "It's Buttons!" she cried as she pulled her light blue T-shirt over her head and rushed down the stairs.

"Dad! Dad!" Nancy shouted from the front hall. "Come quick!"

Nancy Drew and the Clue Crew

#3

Pony Problems

By Carolyn Keene

Illustrated by Macky Pamintuan

Aladdin Paperbacks
New York London Toronto Sydney

CONTENTS

Chapter One: Petting Ponies · · · 1

Chapter Two: Pony's Petunias · · · 12

Chapter Three: Nancy's Notebook · · · 20

Chapter Four: Collecting Clues · · · 29

Chapter Five: Painted Pony · · · 39

Chapter Six: So Many Suspects · · · 50

Chapter Seven: New News · · · 55

Chapter Eight: Cookies and Clues · · · 61

Chapter Nine: Thinking Thoughts · · · 66

Chapter Ten: Case Closed · · · 72

Pony Problems

ChaPTER ONE

Petting Ponies

"I can't believe you're having a turkey sandwich again today." Eight-year-old Nancy Drew shook her head at her best friend Bess. The two girls were sitting together at a long white table in the River Heights Elementary School cafeteria.

"I like turkey," Bess Marvin replied, slowly opening her brown bag and peeking in. "Hey!" Her blond hair swung into her face as she suddenly turned back to Nancy. "How'd you know I was having a turkey sandwich? My lunch bag was closed." Bess pushed her hair out of her eyes.

Just then, Nancy's other best friend, Georgia

Fayne, showed up. George was also Bess's cousin. Even though they were all in the same class, George had stopped to turn in an extra credit math assignment before coming to lunch.

George plopped down on the bench across from Nancy and Bess. She dropped her lunch box on the table. "Nancy probably just guessed," George said, pinning one brown eye on Bess. "I mean, you've had a turkey sandwich every day this week. Since it's Friday, it's easy to guess that you'd have it again today."

"Nancy never guesses," Bess reminded George. "She uses clues to figure stuff out." The girls turned to look at Nancy, who simply smiled.

"It doesn't take a detective to solve this mystery," Nancy remarked. "Bess is the only one I know who likes ketchup on her turkey sandwich." Pointing at the bottom of Bess's lunch bag, Nancy showed Bess the light red stain on the brown paper. "Your mom must have gotten a little ketchup on the bag when she was making your lunch."

Bess turned the bag to look. "I love ketchup so much. Maybe when I finish the sandwich, I'll eat the bag."

The girls laughed.

Nancy winked. "The case of Bess's lunch is now closed," she said with a shrug.

"Not much of a mystery," George commented. "Wouldn't it be great if we had a real case to solve?"

Nancy Drew and her friends loved to solve mysteries. They called themselves the Clue Crew and had a detective headquarters in Nancy's bedroom. Working together, the girls had already solved a couple of good cases and were ready to jump into a new investigation. If only something interesting would happen . . .

"It would be fun to solve another mystery," Nancy agreed. She opened her own lunch box and took out some peanut butter crackers. "But it seems like it's going to be a quiet weekend.

Do you both want to come over tomorrow morning?" she asked her friends. "My dad said he'd take us to fly kites in the park, if you want."

"Sounds good," George said, before eating a spoonful of her yogurt. "Maybe I'll do an Internet search to check out which way the wind will be blowing in River Heights tomorrow." George liked computers and was always sharing interesting facts with her friends.

Bess rolled her eyes. "I bet I can find the same information on my new wireless radio. I built it from old parts I found in that junk shop on East Town Road. My mom took me there last week." Bess loved gadgets. Her hobby was building new stuff out of old pieces.

"It really doesn't matter which way the wind is blowing," Nancy cut in before the cousins began to argue over which was a better weather checker—the Internet or the radio. "Just bring your kites and be there at nine o'clock."

While they were having dessert, Bess asked, "Did you hear about the brown and white speckled pony Ms. Waters found in her garden yesterday?"

George's short brown hair bobbed up and down when she laughed. "My mom said she saw Ms. Waters running down the street in her nightgown, waving her arms and shouting about how the pony was eating her flowers."

"The whole idea cracks me up!" Bess exclaimed. "I mean, she's the librarian. She's always saying 'shhh' and telling us to be quiet. It's hard to imagine her running down the street screaming. My ribs hurt from laughing every time I think about it."

"Ms. Waters sure does love her garden." Nancy giggled. She tucked a strand of her shoulder-length reddish hair behind her ear. "I heard that the day before yesterday, Mr. Geffington found the same pony standing outside the post office. It was eating a bush," Nancy added. She took a sip of milk. "And before that, on Tuesday, the pony was discovered at the movies."

"Was it eating popcorn?" George snickered at

the thought of the pony having a snack.

"Nah," Bess put in. "It was munching leaves off that big sycamore tree in front of the theater."

"That's one hungry pony," George commented. "Does anyone know who it belongs to?" George's eyes lit up as she considered that there might be a mystery to solve.

"Buttons is Mr. Johnson's Shetland pony," a voice said from behind Nancy. The girls turned to see Stacy Quinn headed their way. Stacy was in Mrs. Bailey's third-grade class at River Heights Elementary. Stacy's long brown hair swung as she walked. "I couldn't help but overhear," Stacy continued as she sat down with the three friends at the lunch table. "You guys are talking pretty loudly."

Nancy grinned widely as a question popped into her head. "How do you know the pony's name?"

Stacy reached into the back pocket of her jeans and pulled out a picture. She handed it to Nancy. "See?" she said, pointing at herself in the photograph. "That's me standing next to Buttons." In the picture, Nancy saw Stacy wearing a T-shirt that said "Horse Crazy." She had her hair pulled back and tied with a floppy bow. Her arm was wrapped around a small pony. The pony was a little shorter than Stacy.

Nancy handed the picture to Bess as Stacy went on, "Ponies are amazing animals. I know all about them. But Shetland ponies are the best kind. When I heard there was one at the new petting zoo just outside town, I begged my mom to take me there. Shetland ponies are small. Even when they're grown up, they stay little. I *love* Shetland ponies."

Bess gave the photo to George so she could look at the pony. It had a flowing mane and a bushy tail. Stacy was holding an apple in the picture and smiling like she'd never been so happy in her life.

"All week I've been working as a volunteer at Johnson's Petting Zoo," Stacy shared. "Mr. Johnson lets me come after school. I brush Buttons's mane and feed him apples."

"Like in the picture?" George asked, handing the photo back to Stacy.

Stacy took the photo and said, "Yeah. Buttons always acts like he's hungry. Mr. Johnson only lets me give him one apple a day, but I bet he'd eat more. If Buttons was my pony, I'd give him all the apples he ever wanted." Sighing, Stacy put the photo back in her pocket.

"Buttons keeps escaping from the petting zoo. I think he's looking for food." She went on to explain, "There's an apple tree in my front yard, but Buttons hasn't found it yet. He's too busy eating other people's bushes and gardens. But someday soon, Buttons will discover my tree. When he does, I won't call Mr. Johnson to pick him up. I'll just keep Buttons. He's a great pony. I wish he was mine!" Then, without waiting for Nancy or the other girls to ask her any more questions, Stacy got up and walked away.

"Well, that was kind of strange," Bess said as Stacy left the cafeteria.

"Maybe—," George began, scrunching up her face as she thought.

"I know what you're thinking," Nancy interrupted, pointing her finger at George. "You think that the Clue Crew should investigate how Buttons is getting out of the petting zoo. And find out if Stacy has anything to do with it."

"You're such a good detective," George said with a laugh. "What was your first clue?"

"I didn't need any clues, because I was thinking the same thing." Nancy raised her eyebrows and smiled.

"Do you think we should ask Mr. Johnson if he wants us to investigate?" Bess questioned.

"We can start gathering clues and make a list of suspects," George suggested. "Once he hears the Clue Crew is on the case, he'll definitely want our help!"

"Let's get started." A faraway look clouded Nancy's eyes. "I suppose we should go to the petting zoo, but we're going to need a ride." She jumped up from the bench so suddenly she banged her knees on the bottom of the table. "I know!" Nancy cheered as she bent down to rub her sore knees. "Instead of flying kites in the park, I'll ask my dad to take us to Johnson's Petting Zoo tomorrow."

"That's a great idea," Bess said as she carefully

took the scraps of her turkey sandwich and tucked them back into her lunch bag.

"Aren't you going to throw away your trash?" George asked her cousin.

Bess grinned. "I was thinking that if Buttons is always hungry, maybe he'll like turkey with ketchup. I'm going to leave the rest of my sandwich outside tonight and see if Buttons comes to my house."

"You're goofy." George giggled. "But if there's a pony on your lawn in the morning, you'd better call me right away."

"Hmm," Nancy said thoughtfully, "I wonder where Buttons will pop up tomorrow."

Chapter Two

Pony's Petunias

Saturday morning after breakfast, Nancy was getting dressed when she heard a strange sound outside her window. Looking out, she saw the cutest, shaggiest little pony standing on her front lawn! "It's Buttons!" she cried as she pulled her light blue T-shirt over her head and rushed down the stairs.

"Dad! Dad!" Nancy shouted from the front hall. "Come quick!" Her voice echoed down the long hallway.

Mr. Drew appeared from the kitchen, holding a cup of coffee in his hand. "What's the emergency, Nancy?" he asked, looking concerned.

Nancy's housekeeper, Hannah Gruen, peeked her head out from behind Mr. Drew. Hannah had lived with the Drew family since Nancy was only three years old. She cared for Nancy like she was her own daughter. "Are you bleeding?" Hannah held up a box of Band-Aids. "I was worried when I heard you scream."

Everyone knew that Nancy was a little clumsy. She had a bad habit of bumping into stuff and getting scratches and bruises.

"I'm fine," Nancy told Hannah. "And it's not exactly an emergency." She looked at her dad. "But it *is* exciting news!" Nancy opened the front door of their house so that the adults could see outside.

Buttons was on the grass, having a little snack from the flowerbed.

"My garden!" Hannah exclaimed. "That horse is eating my petunias!"

Nancy laughed. "He's

not a horse, Hannah. Buttons is a Shetland pony."

"Well, then," Hannah complained, "that Shetland pony is eating my petunias."

Nancy filled her dad and Hannah in on who owned Buttons and the pony's adventures around town.

Before Mr. Drew went inside to call Mr. Johnson, he warned Nancy not to touch the pony. "Just keep an eye on Buttons in case he walks away," Mr. Drew said. "Even though he seems like a nice pony, I don't want you to approach him. Let's let Mr. Johnson take care of Buttons."

"What about my flowers?" Hannah asked. "Buttons will eat them all!"

"Nancy will help you plant some new petunias next week," Mr. Drew said. "Let's get Buttons home safely first and worry about the flowers later."

Nancy was sitting on her front porch watching Buttons eat a pink flower when Bess and George came up the sidewalk.

"Oh!" Nancy rushed over to keep the girls

from crossing on the grass. "With all the excitement, I forgot to call you," she apologized. "Buttons must not like ketchup. He chose Hannah's flowers over your sandwich," she told Bess. Nancy pointed to where Buttons was standing. The girls were careful to keep their distance as Mr. Drew had asked. They went up to the house and sat together on the porch.

"I bet Buttons would love ketchup if he tried it," Bess said with a shrug. "Maybe if we get a little, we can put some on that purple petunia and see—," she began, but George interrupted, saying, "Look, here comes Mr. Johnson now."

A white truck pulled up in front of the house. The truck was pulling a small pony trailer. Painted on the side of the trailer, in big, bold, yellow letters, were the words: JOHNSON'S PETTING ZOO. And beneath that in smaller green letters: COME PET OUR ANIMALS AND RIDE OUR PONY.

"DAD!" Nancy hollered at the top of her lungs. "Mr. Johnson's here!"

"You don't have to shout," Mr. Drew said as he came out of the house to greet Mr. Johnson. The owner of the petting zoo was a bear of a man. He looked about the same age as Mr. Drew, but Mr. Drew was tall and thin, with plenty of brown hair on his head. Mr. Johnson was round and balding. He wore a white shirt with blue jeans held up by bright blue suspenders. There was a red bandanna tied around his neck, and he wore a straw cowboy hat on his head.

The girls followed Mr. Drew out to the truck, curious to hear what Mr. Johnson would say.

"Thanks for calling me." Mr. Johnson shook hands with Mr. Drew. "That woman yesterday, when she found Buttons in her garden, she didn't call. She just chased him down the street in her nightgown while she banged two pans together. I finally found Buttons a few blocks away, near the pizza parlor, eating berries off a mulberry bush."

"Good thing the pizza parlor wasn't open yet," George remarked, remembering how Stacy had said that Buttons was always hungry.

"Crazy pony," Mr. Johnson muttered. Opening the trailer, he grabbed a long piece of lead rope out of a box. "Why won't you just stay in the zoo?" he asked the pony as he slipped the rope around Buttons's neck and tied a knot.

Buttons neighed in reply.

Mr. Johnson sighed. "All righty there," he said as he pulled Buttons away from the flowers. "That's enough snacking for today. You're supposed to eat healthy hay like the rest of the animals!" Mr. Johnson lowered a ramp on the trailer and pushed Buttons inside, closing the door behind the pony. He double-checked the lock on the trailer door, saying, "We can't have you escaping while I'm driving you home."

Once Buttons was ready to go, Mr. Johnson

came over to talk to Mr. Drew and the girls. "Sorry for the trouble this morning," he said, lowering his eyes. "I'll gladly pay for the damaged flowers if you'd like."

"Don't worry about the flowers," Mr. Drew said. "We're just glad that Buttons is going back to the petting zoo where he belongs."

"I wish I could keep him there," Mr. Johnson said. "No matter how many times I check the lock on the pen, he still escapes every night." Rubbing his forehead with his fingers, he added, "It's a mystery to me how that pony is getting out of the zoo."

George leaned over and whispered in Bess's ear. Then Bess whispered the same message in Nancy's. Nancy nodded.

"The Clue Crew would love to help you solve this mystery," Nancy told Mr. Johnson. "We can come to the petting zoo right now. Can't we, Dad?"

"I thought you girls wanted to spend the day at Bluff View Park," Mr. Drew said. Then he noticed that Bess and George weren't carrying anything in their hands. "I see." He nodded slightly. "You already knew about Buttons's escape act. You girls were thinking about solving this one, eh? I bet you were going to ask me to take you to the petting zoo today, weren't you?"

Nancy was surprised. "How'd you guess?" she asked.

"I might be only a lawyer, but I'm also the father of River Heights's greatest detective." Mr. Drew smiled. "I know a clue when I see one, and you girls don't have your kites with you."

"That's good detective work, Dad," Nancy replied.

Mr. Drew laughed, leaned over, and ruffled his daughter's hair. "I've learned a few things from you, Nancy Drew!" He turned to Mr. Johnson, saying, "If it's okay with you, I'll bring the girls to the petting zoo so they can investigate this mystery."

Mr. Johnson didn't even hesitate. He gave the girls a big smile and said, "You're hired!"

CHAPTER THREE

Nancy's Notebook

Even though it was Saturday morning, there weren't many people at the petting zoo. Nancy wondered why.

Before they'd left the house, she had run up to her bedroom to get her new purple notebook and matching purple pencil. They were a present from Bess and George on her last birthday. Purple was Nancy's favorite color, and solving mysteries was her favorite thing to do. The gift was perfect.

Opening the notebook, Nancy wrote, *How is Buttons getting out of the petting zoo?* On the next page, she made two columns. One for clues, and one for suspects.

Under suspects, she wrote down *Stacy Quinn.*

Stacy said that if Buttons came to her house, she'd keep him. She also said that Buttons loved apples, and she had an apple tree in her yard. Maybe Stacy was letting Buttons out, hoping he'd come over.

"Nancy, hurry up," Bess called from inside the animal pen. She and George were excited to pet the animals and had rushed ahead. "Come see the baby chicks. They are sooo cute."

Nancy closed her notebook, slipped it into her pocket, and headed toward her friends. She was still thinking about Stacy and Buttons and apple trees. In fact, Nancy was thinking so hard, she wandered off the cement path and tripped over a pretty big rock.

"Oof," Nancy grunted as she stumbled forward and fell to the ground.

"Are you okay?" Careful not to let any animals out, Bess opened the pen door, shut it behind her, then hurried over to Nancy.

"I'm fine," Nancy told Bess. Bess gave her a hand up. "Good thing my dad was over talking to Mr. Johnson. He's always telling me to watch where I'm walking. If Hannah was here, she'd be putting Band-Aids all over me, whether I needed them or not."

Nancy wiped the dirt off her pants. "I really can't help being clumsy. Sometimes I just start thinking and my feet turn left when they should stay straight. . . ." Her voice trailed off when she saw the huge animal pen in front of her.

Sure she'd looked up when Bess had called her name, but she had been so deep in thought she hadn't really noticed the bright red, white, and blue painted rails of the tall, split-rail fence.

"Wow!" Nancy exclaimed, taking it all in.

Moving closer, she discovered that the top of the fence was slightly higher than her head. There was chicken wire between the rails so no animal could slip out.

Roomy bunny cages stood along one fence wall. A separate area for the chickens had a little pond. Buttons was wandering around, hanging out with the goats and sheep.

There was also a large shady area with plenty of room where the bigger animals could go if it was too sunny or when it rained.

Nancy opened the large, swinging gate just enough for her and Bess to slip inside.

George rushed over. "Nancy, are you hurt? I saw you fall."

"Not a scratch," Nancy replied.

George was happy to hear that Nancy was fine and handed her a quarter. "I brought some coins from my allowance," she explained. "Do you want to buy some goat and sheep food?" There were a few food machines hanging on one side of the pen fence.

"Sure. Thanks." Nancy took the quarter and walked over to a goat and sheep food machine. Buttons was standing in front of the machine, bumping it with his nose and neighing.

Nancy hadn't been allowed to touch Buttons when he was on her lawn at home, but now that he was back at the petting zoo, Mr. Drew said it was okay.

Remembering that Mr. Johnson said Buttons should be eating hay, Nancy looked around for a bale. It wasn't far, so Nancy headed over to it. Buttons followed her. "I know you're hoping I'll feed you some goat food," Nancy told the pony. "Wouldn't you like some healthy hay instead?" Nancy took a handful of clean hay off the bale. "Here." She held her hand out for the pony. "This is for you."

Buttons stared at the hay, wiggled his nose at Nancy, and then walked away.

I don't think Buttons likes hay, Nancy said to herself. She quickly opened her notebook and wrote, *Buttons doesn't like hay* in the clue column.

Nancy decided she'd feed the goats later. Now that she had one clue, she was excited to search for more. Tucking the quarter into her pocket, Nancy went over to join Bess and George.

Bess and George were standing near the gate talking to Mr. Drew and Mr. Johnson. Mr. Drew was not an animal lover and was shooing away a goat, who was nibbling on the side of his shirt. The goat didn't want to leave Mr. Drew alone! Finally, Mr. Johnson got some goat pellets and threw them a distance away. The goat hustled off to have a snack.

"I bought the petting zoo a few weeks ago," Mr. Johnson explained. "Before that, I worked at a bank in Hailey Town." Nancy had been to Hailey Town before. It was about a twenty-minute drive south of River Heights.

"I didn't like working in a bank," Mr. Johnson went on. "I always dreamed about having my own petting zoo. When this old farm was for sale, I bought it and we moved out here. I purchased all the animals and built the fence myself." He pointed at the small red barn behind the zoo fence. "I built the barn, too."

Then Mr. Johnson pointed to a brick house with a nice porch and a swing set on the side. "The only thing I didn't build is our house. It came with the farm."

The goat came back and was bugging Mr. Drew for more food. Nancy handed her dad the quarter George had given her. Mr. Drew bought a little food and threw it into the center of the pen like he'd seen Mr. Johnson do. The goat ran after it.

"My wife and I love it here." Mr. Johnson looked around. "Business could be better, however. I think that if more people knew how great Buttons was, more kids would come to ride him and pet the other animals. Buttons is a Shetland pony, you see." Nancy, Bess, and George all nodded. They already knew that. "Shetlands are great. They have sweet personalities, love kids, and get along with all the other animals," Mr. Johnson finished.

Suddenly, a loud, grumpy sound came from the red barn behind the pen. It was a cross between a sigh and a snort.

"Do you have pigs at the zoo?" Bess asked Mr. Johnson.

The zoo owner wrinkled his forehead and raised his eyebrows. "No. Just the sheep, goats, bunnies, and chickens." He looked across toward the barn. "And one escaping pony."

"Are any animals in the barn?" George asked, staring in the direction where the sound came from.

"No, they're all out here," Mr. Johnson answered. "The barn is really just a storage shed. No animals are allowed in the barn. They all live in the pen."

Suddenly the barn door slammed shut. The angry noise made such a racket that all the animals stopped eating and looked up. Nancy,

George, and Bess looked up too. They saw a girl about their own age, with short, black, curly hair. The girl ran out of the barn toward Mr. Johnson's house.

"Who's that?" Nancy asked Mr. Johnson.

They watched the girl fly up the porch steps and disappear into the brick house. "That's my daughter, Amanda," Mr. Johnson answered with a long, unhappy sigh.

Chapter Four

Collecting Clues

"Amanda seems supermad about something," Bess whispered to George and Nancy. "Slamming the barn door and stomping off like that. I'd like to ask her about the escaping pony, but I don't think she'll want to talk to us right now."

"I think you're right," Nancy agreed. "Let's look around for some clues, and maybe we can ask Amanda about the pony later."

Nancy opened her notebook and showed Bess and George the pages she'd started.

"This is great!" George cheered after looking at the one clue and one suspect on Nancy's list. "Tomorrow we can come over to your house and

I'll copy everything we find into a computer file."

Bess wanted to go check out the padlock on the animal pen gate. The girls asked Mr. Johnson if he could show them exactly how he locked up every night.

"You girls sure do take this detective work seriously," he commented as he walked with them to the large hinged gate.

"Yes, we do, Mr. Johnson," Bess answered. "The Clue Crew is eager to solve this mystery for you."

"Well, then," he began, "every night I give the animals a new bale of hay. Then I count them before I shut the gate. Lately, I've been taking special care to check that Buttons is inside the pen. He always is." Mr. Johnson closed the gate and hooked a small latch. After that, he slipped a large padlock through a hole drilled in the latch. Then he secured the lock.

"Can I see the lock?" Bess asked, stepping forward.

"Be my guest," Mr. Johnson said as he moved aside.

Bess pulled at the lock. It was firmly closed. She tugged some more, but the lock wouldn't open. "Can I check out the key?" she asked Mr. Johnson. Bess took the key and opened the lock. She shut the lock tightly and handed the key back to Mr. Johnson. "Does anyone else have a key?"

"No," Mr. Johnson replied. "I have the only one." He unlocked the gate and put the key in his pocket. "I take the key home at night and hang it on a hook in the kitchen. Every morning I get the key off the hook to open the petting zoo for the day."

"Has the key ever been missing?" Nancy asked him.

"Never," he said with a shake of his head. "The key is always right where I put it."

"Hmm." Bess bit her bottom lip. "Nancy, will you write down in your notebook that the lock works and that the key hangs on a hook at night?" She paused, then said, "Maybe we need another column for stuff we should remember."

"Good idea." Nancy made a column and added the two facts. She also wrote a reminder to think about why there weren't very many people at the petting zoo on such a beautiful spring day. Then she closed her notebook.

"There must be more clues around here somewhere." Bess quickly surveyed the pen and the animals but didn't immediately see anything out of place.

The three friends decided to split up and search around.

"Over here," George called after a few minutes. Bess and Nancy hurried to where George stood outside the fenced pen. Through the rails, she pointed at a bale of hay sitting near the fence. A goat was standing on top of the bale, eating. Yellowish-green strands of hay were hanging out of its mouth as it chewed.

"It's hay," Nancy said. "There's hay all over the ground. That's not a clue."

George pointed out that the bale of hay was half-eaten.

"I still don't understand what the clue is," Nancy prodded.

"Well," George said. "If Mr. Johnson puts a bale of hay inside the fence every night and the animals eat it, why is there so much hay outside the fence too?" She pointed at the ground nearby.

"You're right!" Nancy exclaimed. "It *is* a clue!" She bent low to the ground to examine the evidence. Even though they were standing outside the fence, there was hay all over. "Do you think the goats, sheep, and pony can spit this far?" Nancy asked, then took a few big steps to where the last scraps of hay were lying on the ground.

"These aren't *camels,*" Bess remarked. When no one laughed, she explained, "Camels are known to be big spitters. I read it in a book at school."

George laughed. "I get it now. But are goats big spitters too?"

"I didn't read about that." Bess shrugged. "I can check on Monday when we get to school."

"Maybe Mr. Johnson simply dropped bits of hay when he carried the bale into the pen," Nancy suggested. "But we should write it down anyway." She opened her notebook and wrote in the clue column: *Hay outside the animal pen.*

Just as Nancy was closing the notebook, Bess asked, "Isn't that Amanda Johnson over there?" On the other side of the pen, they could see a girl in white painter's pants standing on a small ladder, leaning over the top rung of the fence.

"It sure is," Nancy answered. The girls decided to go talk to Amanda about the pony's disappearances. "Maybe she's seen something suspicious," Nancy said as they made their way around the pen.

Amanda was busy painting. She was smearing a new coat of red paint on the top rung of the animal pen fence.

"Hi," Nancy greeted Amanda. "We hear you're new to town. I'm Nancy Drew and these are my friends, Bess Marvin and George Fayne."

Amanda didn't get off the ladder. She didn't even look down at the girls. She just kept on painting.

"Welcome to River Heights," Bess said, reaching up and putting out her hand for Amanda to shake.

Amanda didn't shake Bess's hand. She kept painting.

George began to explain that they were investigating the mystery of Buttons's visits to town.

"She won't talk to you," a voice behind them

said. The girls turned to see Stacy standing behind them. "I've tried a thousand times. She won't talk to me either," she continued.

Nancy felt weird talking about Amanda in front of her, but since Amanda wouldn't say anything, Nancy asked Stacy, "Why won't she talk?"

Stacy gave Amanda a second to answer for herself, but Amanda simply dipped her brush in the red paint and silently swiped it along the fence.

"Mr. Johnson told me that Amanda doesn't talk to any kids in River Heights. Not here at the petting zoo and not at school, either."

"Is she sick?" George asked.

"Nah. She just doesn't talk. That's all. She's refused to say one word to any kids since the day she moved to River Heights. I guess she doesn't want any new friends." Stacy shrugged and pulled an apple out of her jacket pocket. "I still try every day." Stacy turned to Amanda and said, "Hi. Want to go feed Buttons with me?" She held out the apple so Amanda could see it.

When Amanda didn't answer, Stacy said, "We have the exact same conversation every single day. I ask her to join me and she doesn't answer. I keep hoping that one of these times, she's going to take the apple and come into the pen with me. Until then, I'm feeding Buttons on my own. I just love that pony!" She called, "See ya!" over her shoulder as she ran toward the pen.

When Stacy was gone, Nancy stepped closer to Amanda and said, "We'd like to be your friends." Bess and George nodded their heads, totally agreeing.

Amanda didn't answer. She turned her eyes away so that Nancy couldn't see them. Then, even though she hadn't finished the fence rail, Amanda put the lid on her paint, tucked her paintbrush into her overalls pocket, picked up the small ladder, and walked away without saying a single word.

CHAPTER FIVE

Painted Pony

The phone at Nancy's house rang early Sunday morning.

"Hello?" Nancy picked up the phone after Hannah told her the call was for her.

"Nancy?" It was George. "You'd better come over ASAP. You aren't going to believe who is standing on my front lawn!"

"Is it Bess?" Nancy was kidding. She knew right away it wasn't Bess. George never got this excited about her cousin.

"No, it's Buttons!" George thought Nancy was serious. She paused for a second as she thought about Nancy's question. "You were kidding, right? You knew it was Buttons." Nancy giggled and George laughed in return

"Gotcha!" Nancy said.

"I'm going to call Bess now," George said.

"Okay. I'm on my way!" Nancy hung up, grabbed her purple notebook and pencil, and hurried downstairs. She paused to get permission to go to George's. The very second her dad said it was okay, Nancy fled out the door and ran the three short blocks to George's house.

"Hi, Bess. Hi, George. Hi, Buttons," Nancy greeted the gang as she hurried up the front walkway. Bess and George were standing off to the side, watching the pony eat leaves off the Faynes' willow tree.

"What are you doing here?' Nancy asked Buttons. Buttons neighed and chewed off a few more leaves.

"I wish Buttons could tell us how he's getting out of the petting zoo," Nancy said. "It sure would make this an easy mystery to solve." Buttons neighed again as if he understood and was trying to tell.

Just then, Bess noticed a strange red marking

on one of Buttons's back hooves. She pointed it out to George and Nancy. They stepped in a little closer to get a better look.

"Girls!" Mrs. Fayne called from inside the house, through the kitchen window. "Stay back from that pony. I know he likes kids and is nice at the farm, but you need to be careful when Mr. Johnson isn't around. I've already called him. He's on his way."

"But Mom—," George began.

Mrs. Fayne didn't repeat herself. She just shot them a warning look.

"No really, Mom." George moved back from the pony and closer to the kitchen window. "We were checking Buttons's hoof. It looks like he's bleeding."

Mrs. Fayne came out of the house, drying her hands on a small towel. Slowly she approached the pony, talking softly and making a nice clicking sound with her tongue.

"I didn't know your mom knew about ponies," Nancy told George.

"She grew up on a farm in Ohio," George answered. "Sometimes she talks about how much she misses living on a farm."

Mrs. Fayne put a soothing hand on Buttons's side, being careful to stay in front of his hind hooves. She bent low to take a look.

"That's not blood," Mrs. Fayne remarked at last. "Hooves are hard and wouldn't bleed even if he did break one. There is no scratch on his

leg." She looked closer at the red mark. "That looks like paint."

The girls were surprised.

"Paint?" Bess cried. "Like the red paint Amanda Johnson was using yesterday!"

Nancy immediately pulled out her notebook and pencil. In the clue column, she wrote down: *Red paint on Buttons's hoof.*

"Maybe Amanda got paint on the ground and Buttons stepped in it?" George asked.

"I don't think so," Bess replied. "Amanda was outside the fence painting. Buttons was inside with the other animals."

"Weird." Nancy tapped her temple with the pencil eraser. Since Mrs. Fayne knew about ponies, Nancy asked her, "Can Shetland ponies jump?"

"Do you think Buttons might have jumped over the petting zoo fence?" Bess cut in. "Maybe he dragged his hoof on the rail at the last second?"

"I was just thinking." Nancy shrugged.

"Jumping would explain the paint. And possibly solve the mystery."

Mrs. Fayne gave Buttons a final pat on the back and stepped away. "We didn't have Shetlands on our farm in Ohio." She came over to where the girls were standing. "I don't know how high Shetlands can jump. They're different from other ponies." A truck engine vroomed as it turned onto George's street. "Here comes Mr. Johnson. Why don't you ask him?"

Mr. Johnson parked the truck and pony trailer in front of George's house. The girls waited for him to get his rope and tie it around Buttons's neck. Before he put the pony in the trailer, Nancy showed him the paint marking on Buttons's hoof.

"Can Shetland ponies jump?" George asked.

"They can," Mr. Johnson answered. For a second, Nancy thought they'd solved the mystery. "But that's why I built the extra-tall fence around the animal pen." Nancy recalled noticing that the fence was above her head. "Shetland ponies can't jump that high," Mr. Johnson said. "Nope. There's no way Buttons jumped over that fence."

The zoo owner put Buttons in the trailer for the ride back to the petting zoo. "Why don't you come back to the petting zoo again today? We're open all day on Sundays, and I have a reporter from the newspaper coming. You can tell her about the Clue Crew and how you are working to solve this mystery."

Mrs. Fayne agreed to take the girls back to the petting zoo as long as she could take George's two-year-old brother Scott along.

"The petting zoo's the perfect place to bring Scott," Mr. Johnson told her. "He's going to love it. And because of the trouble Buttons caused this morning, I'll give him a ride on the pony for free."

"Your brother is a nut," Nancy said to George. George laughed.

Little Scott was riding Buttons, clapping his

hands, totally excited to be on the back of the pony. Mrs. Fayne kept telling him to hold on, and Mr. Johnson repeatedly showed him how to hold on to the pony's long mane. They had gone outside the animal pen and were walking around a small track Mr. Johnson had made just beyond the barn.

The reporter was there. She was taking pictures of Scott on the pony. Nancy had overheard

the reporter ask permission from Mrs. Fayne to take a few pictures for the article.

As soon as Scott's ride was over, Mr. Johnson came and introduced the girls to Sally Walton, the newspaper reporter. "Ms. Walton is going to write a nice long article," Mr. Johnson told them.

"That's right," Ms. Walton agreed. "Once I heard about Buttons and how he keeps escaping, well, I thought, this is a great story!"

She told them that the article would be a whole page with pictures.

"Isn't that terrific?" Mr. Johnson asked, full of excitement. "After people read the article, everyone will want to come see Buttons. He'll be a celebrity. Finally, people will fill up my petting zoo!"

Mr. Johnson told Ms. Walton all about the Clue Crew and how they were helping to solve the mystery.

"I need to talk to Mr. Johnson for a few minutes," Ms. Walton told them. "But will you girls hang around? If it's okay with your parents, I'd love to take some pictures of you for the paper and interview you for the article."

"You bet!" Bess, George, and Nancy said at the exact same time. Mrs. Walton told the girls that their parents would have to fill out permission slips to print their pictures in the newspaper. She handed the forms out and asked the girls to have their parents fax the forms back to her later in the day.

"No problem," Bess said, pocketing her form. George's mom could sign the paper now, since she had brought them to the petting zoo.

Nancy tucked her slip in her pocket too.

"While we're waiting," George suggested, "let's look for more clues."

They were searching around the animal pen for anything that seemed odd or out of place, when Bess stood up suddenly and slapped her hand against her thigh.

Hearing the noise, Nancy and George hurried over.

"Did you find a clue?" Nancy asked.

"No," Bess responded. "But I've been thinking, and I've decided something important." She paused. "Mr. Johnson is a suspect."

Chapter Six

So Many Suspects

Nancy opened her notebook and asked, "What gives you that idea, Bess?"

"Well." Bess bit her lip as she thought. "What if Mr. Johnson is letting Buttons out on purpose? He said the petting zoo isn't doing enough business. I think maybe he let Buttons out so that he could call the newspaper and tell them Buttons is escaping." She nibbled her bottom lip. "I bet the newspaper wouldn't come to see a regular pony. Having an escaping pony could be a good thing for Mr. Johnson and the petting zoo."

Nancy turned to the page in her notebook where she had written a reminder about how there weren't many people at the petting zoo.

She looked around. It was a sunny Sunday and there still weren't very many people visiting.

"I think Bess might be right," Nancy said at last. She wrote Mr. Johnson's name on the suspect list. "Mr. Johnson has the key to the pen's gate. He could be letting Buttons out on purpose."

George scratched her head. "I'm not so sure. I don't think he likes Buttons roaming around town by himself. It's not safe. Plus, he asked us to help him solve the mystery. Suspects usually don't ask for help."

"Good point," Nancy agreed. "But I think we'd better keep him on the suspect list until we're sure."

"Hey, check it out." Bess suddenly pointed off in the distance. "There's Amanda Johnson." Amanda was over at the pen fence, painting the blue rail this time. "Should we try to talk to her again?"

"Let's ask her if she knows about the red paint on Buttons's hoof," George suggested.

When they reached Amanda, she was finished

painting the rail. There was a smudge of blue paint on her nose.

"Please talk to us," Nancy said. "We want to be your friends."

Amanda didn't say anything. She just gathered up her stuff and headed to the barn.

Not willing to give up, the girls walked with her and waited silently while Amanda put her painting supplies away.

As Amanda shut the barn door, George said, "Wouldn't you like to have some friends in River Heights?"

"No." Amanda put her hands on her hips. "I don't want any friends in River Heights." She looked seriously at Nancy, Bess, and George. "I have friends in Hailey Town. I don't like it here. I want to go back there."

"You can talk!" Bess said, surprised. "Oops, I didn't mean to get so excited." She stepped closer to Amanda and said in a soft voice, "I bet if you tried harder you might like River Heights. It's a really nice place."

Tears welled up in Amanda's eyes. She backed away from Bess. "I'll never like it here. No matter what! I never had to paint the fence as a chore in Hailey Town!" She wiped her tears on the back of her hand. "If Buttons would just go away and stay away, no one would come to the petting zoo. Dad would have to sell the farm and we could go back home." And before the girls could say anything to make Amanda feel better, she took off running toward the house.

The girls decided not to follow.

"This isn't going so well," George told Nancy and Bess.

"She doesn't want to be our friend, and we forgot to ask her about the red paint." Bess frowned.

Nancy took a breath and let it out slowly. "Can we be friends with a suspect?" she asked at last.

George squinted curiously at Nancy. "Why is she a suspect?"

Nancy took out her purple notebook and

flipped through the pages. When she found the suspects column, she answered, "Amanda wishes Buttons would go away forever. She knows how important Buttons is to the petting zoo. Maybe she thinks they can move back to Hailey Town if he disappears."

"You think she's letting Buttons out, hoping he'll never come back?" Bess was shocked. "Amanda doesn't seem that mean."

Nancy shrugged. "Maybe she just *really* wants to move back to Hailey Town."

"Amanda could easily get the key to the animal pen off the hook," George added.

Nancy let her eyes drift toward the house. She could now see Amanda on the front porch steps at her house. "I can't believe we already have three suspects. We're getting really close to solving this mystery!"

Chapter Seven

New News

Ms. Walton called the girls together just inside the petting zoo gate. "I have a few questions to ask you," she said. "When did you decide to investigate this mystery?"

Nancy had begun to answer when George's brother Scott ran past. He was chasing a sheep, which was doing its best to run away. Scott and the sheep went around Nancy twice. Then Scott took a shortcut—right between Nancy's legs!

"Oof," Nancy grunted as she stumbled backward in surprise. George caught her just before she hit the ground.

"Sorry," George apologized for her brother. "Scott can be such a maniac sometimes."

"It's okay," Nancy began, "I'm used to tripping, stumbling, bumping into stuff, and falling." She glanced over her shoulder at Scott. "Thanks for catching me, George." Nancy moved her legs closer together so there wasn't any room between them, in case Scott came running by again.

Out of the corner of her eye, George could see that Scott had given up on the sheep and was now chasing a goat. "Poor goat." George shook her head.

The girls laughed.

"Now then," Ms. Walton got back on track. "Tell me

how you heard about the pony popping up in town."

"Well," Bess began this time. "We all heard about Ms. Waters"—Bess began to giggle—"and how she ran down the street in her nightgown." Her eyes began to water, and she wrapped her arms around herself. She was trying to hold back her laughter. "She was chasing—" It was no use. Bess started laughing so hard, she snorted.

George took over the story. "Then, on Saturday, Buttons came to Nancy's house." George would have said more, but Scott hurried by. He was quacking like a duck and pretending to fly. "Mom!" George called to Mrs. Fayne. "Make him stop."

"He's just playing," Mrs. Fayne replied. "He's not hurting anyone."

"He almost hurt Nancy," George complained.

"But I'm okay," Nancy put in.

Mrs. Fayne went over to Scott and told him to calm down.

"I'm a duck," Scott replied. "I live at the zoo." He pointed at the pond and the birds.

"Those are chickens," George told him. "Not ducks."

"Quack," Scott said. "Quack. Quack." He was flapping his arms again. He climbed up on a bale of hay and leaped off. "Quack," he repeated as he landed in the soft hay on the petting zoo floor. He climbed back up to do it

again. "Now I'm a goat," Scott announced, making a *maa* sound.

"Mom," George moaned, "he's still bugging us. We can't finish the interview if Scott keeps interrupting."

"Looks like he's busy now," Mrs. Fayne remarked as Scott struggled to climb back on top of the bale of hay. "I'll keep my little goat over here while you girls talk to Ms. Walton." This time, when Scott jumped, Mrs. Fayne caught him and swung him around. "Maa," she said to her son and set him back on the bale.

Ms. Walton asked the girls a few more questions about the pony. Then she asked them how the investigation was going.

"Pretty good," Nancy responded. She pulled out her purple notebook but didn't open it. "We have a few suspects and a whole bunch of clues."

"How are you going to solve this case?" Ms. Walton asked.

"Well," George answered, "we're going to head over to Nancy's house today. I need to input our notes into the computer. Then we'll work together to solve the mystery."

Just then, Stacy arrived with an apple for Buttons. "Hi," she said to the girls. "Who are you talking to?" Stacy looked at the reporter.

George introduced her to Ms. Walton.

Mr. Johnson walked over to them. "Let's take a picture for the paper!" he said. "It'll be great. After this, everyone will want to come and ride Buttons, the famous pony!"

Bess, George, and Nancy gathered together in the front row for the picture. Buttons was on the side, with Stacy holding his reins, of course. In the back were Mr. Johnson and a very unhappy Amanda, who had been forced to be in the photo.

"Smile," Ms. Walton said, looking though the camera lens.

"Fantastic," Bess grumbled. She leaned over and whispered to George and Nancy, "In tomorrow's newspaper there will be a photo of the Clue Crew standing with their three suspects!"

Chapter Eight

Cookies and Clues

It was Sunday afternoon. The girls were in Nancy's bedroom, talking while George booted up Nancy's computer.

"Detective work is fun," Bess said as she flopped backward onto Nancy's bed. The purple covers were crinkled beneath her. "But it's hard work, too." She grabbed a pillow and hugged it to her chest.

Nancy got out her purple notebook and flipped through the pages.

"Computer's ready," George announced. "I started a new file for this case."

"Great." Nancy looked down at what she'd written. "We have three suspects. Stacy Quinn,

Mr. Johnson, and Amanda Johnson."

From over at Nancy's desk, George stopped typing. "It's hard to think of them as suspects because we really like all of them. It's a bummer to think that one of them is letting Buttons out of the animal pen."

There was a knock on Nancy's door.

"Come in," Nancy called instead of answering the door herself.

"Hello, girls," Hannah said as she walked into the room, carrying a white plastic tray. "Why are you looking so sad?"

"We aren't sad," Nancy answered. "We just like all our suspects."

"Take a break," Hannah said as she set the tray on top of Nancy's dresser. "I made cookies. Eat. Drink some milk. Things aren't always what they seem. Did you review your clues?"

"Not yet," Nancy answered. "We were talking about the suspects first."

"After your snack, check your clues." Hannah walked to the door. "You girls know," she reminded them as she closed the door behind her, "that good detectives always think about their clues."

Each girl ate two chocolate cookies and drank a glass of milk. Full and happy, they were ready to get back to work.

"Clues," Nancy said, reading the column in her notebook. "Buttons doesn't like hay. There is a lot of hay outside the pen. Then, there's the red paint on Buttons's hoof."

Suddenly, Bess sat up on the bed. "I just realized something. Stacy can't be a suspect. The key to the lock is kept in Mr. Johnson's house. She doesn't have a way to open the gate."

"Good thinking," Nancy cheered. "I think we should go talk to Stacy again. Let's ask her if she's letting the pony out. That way we can cross her off our list for sure."

As a rule, the girls were only allowed to walk five blocks from Nancy's house. Luckily, Stacy lived three blocks away.

The girls were there a few minutes later.

George knocked. "Who's there?" Stacy asked through the closed door.

"Nancy Drew and the Clue Crew," Nancy replied. Stacy immediately opened the door.

"Hi." Nancy didn't waste any time. "Are you letting Buttons out at night? You said you would keep him if he showed up at you house."

"Sure, I'd love to keep him, but that's just a dream." Stacy laughed. "Buttons belongs to Mr. Johnson and has a good life at the petting zoo. I can visit there any time I want. Sure I wish Buttons lived at my house, but where would I put him? In the living room?"

"He'd probably enjoy staying in the kitchen," Bess put in, and all the girls chuckled.

Nancy thought of an important question that Stacy could easily answer. "Mrs. Fayne told us that Shetland ponies are different from other ponies. Why?"

Stacy didn't even pause to think about the answer. She quickly said, "In many ways Shetlands are more like goats than ponies." Just then, Stacy's mom called from upstairs. "I'd better go. We're leaving to visit my grandparents on the other side of town. I have to change into nicer clothes. See ya at school tomorrow."

Back in Nancy's bedroom, Bess suggested, "Let's cross her off the suspect list." Nancy got out her notebook and put a purple line though Stacy's name. George deleted her name from the computer file.

"Only two suspects left," George remarked. "If Stacy isn't letting Buttons go, who is?"

CHAPTER NINE

Thinking Thoughts

Monday morning the phone rang at Nancy's house. Nancy was already awake and ready for school, even though it wasn't time to leave yet. All night her brain had been working on the mystery. She hadn't slept very well.

Nancy was comparing ponies and goats. Buttons made a neighing sound, like a pony. He was short like a goat, but other than that, he looked like a pony. Goats ate anything. So did Buttons. Except hay. Buttons didn't like hay.

Her head was spinning from thinking so much.

When the phone rang, she decided that since she was up, she'd answer it.

"Hello, Drew residence," Nancy said politely, just like Hannah had taught her.

"Nancy?" It was Bess. "You aren't going to believe this!"

Nancy glanced at the clock. It was really early. "Should I guess? Because I bet I know why you're calling. There's a four-legged visitor at your house, right?"

"Yes!" Bess confirmed. "Buttons is eating our grass! Right now!"

"I wish I had time to come over," Nancy said. "It might be early, but Dad would never let me rush over there before school."

"George's mom said no too," Bess replied.

"Did you look around for clues?" Nancy asked. "Like when we found the paint on his hoof at George's."

"Of course," Bess said. Nancy could imagine Bess looking the pony over, searching for something unusual. "I didn't find anything. Mr. Johnson must have washed off that red paint mark. This morning, nothing looks suspicious."

"Hmmm," Nancy said, then went silent.

"Nancy?" Bess called into the phone. "Nancy? Are you still there? Talk to me. I can hear you breathing. Earth to Nancy."

Suddenly, Nancy snapped out of it. "I'm here. Sorry. I was thinking."

"Think later," Bess advised. "I'd better go. Mr. Johnson just arrived to pick Buttons up. I'll see you at school."

All day at school, Nancy was thinking about the mystery. She paid attention in class, but between classes and at lunch, she was constantly bumping into stuff, walking into walls, and tripping on the ends of her shoes. By the time recess came, Bess and George were afraid to leave her alone. She might hurt herself.

"Oof," Nancy said as she banged her elbow on the ladder leading up to the monkey bars.

"Okay," Bess told Nancy. "You'd better tell us what you're thinking, because school's almost over and we can't protect you forever."

"Why are you protecting me?" Nancy asked, rubbing her sore elbow. She hadn't noticed that Bess and George had been following her around all day.

"We have to save you from yourself!" George answered. "Your head is stuck at Johnson's Petting Zoo."

"That's not such a bad place to be stuck." Bess smiled. "It's superfun there. Did you see the article and photographs in today's newspaper?"

Just like Ms. Walton had said, there was a full-page article in the paper. Nancy had seen the picture of herself, Bess, and George with Stacy, Mr. Johnson, and Amanda. Next to that, there was also a smaller picture of Scott riding Buttons.

Bess grinned. "Remember yesterday when Scott was jumping off the hay pretending he was a duck? It was annoying at the time, but now it seems pretty funny."

"Quack," said George. "My brother can be such a spaz sometimes!"

"Maa," said Bess. "I'm a goat!" She held two fingers like horns on her head. "Maa."

"Quack, quack." George responded, flapping her arms and running in circles around Bess and Nancy.

"That's it!" Suddenly, Nancy's eyes grew wide. "Thanks to the both of you, I think I just figured out this mystery."

"What did we do?" George stopped quacking.

"How did we help?" Bess stopped bleating.

"What are you doing after school today?" Nancy asked Bess and George.

They didn't have any plans, except homework.

"Good." Nancy seemed very happy. "Do your homework right away. I'm going to ask Hannah if she'll drive us over to the petting zoo."

"Aren't you going to fill us in?" Bess and George asked together.

"Later," Nancy said as the school bell rang. It was time to go back to class. "Meet me at my house at four o'clock. When we get to the petting zoo, I'll tell you the answer to the mystery."

CHAPTER TEN

Case Closed

When Nancy, Bess, and George arrived at the petting zoo, Stacy was already there. She was brushing Buttons's mane.

Amanda was there too. She was filling the water dishes in the bunny cages.

Nancy went to get Mr. Johnson. She told him she had something important to share.

"What is it?" Mr. Johnson asked. "Did you solve the mystery?"

Nancy smiled and said, "I won't tell until everyone is together."

They gathered inside the animal pen, under the shaded area.

"I know how Buttons is getting out," Nancy

began. "At first I thought maybe Stacy was letting him out, but then, Bess realized that Stacy couldn't possibly get the key to the gate."

George added, "We asked Stacy anyway. She said she didn't do it."

"Right!" Nancy punched the air. "But Stacy gave us a new clue."

"I did?" Stacy asked. "I didn't know I gave you a clue."

"You said something really important," Nancy told her. "You said that Shetlands are like goats." Stacy smiled. She was glad she'd been helpful, even if she didn't quite understand.

Nancy turned to Amanda. "We thought *you* might be letting Buttons out because if Buttons disappeared, you might get to move back to Hailey Town."

"I didn't let him out," Amanda said. "Really. I might not like it here, but I know how much my dad loves the farm. I'd never do anything to hurt him."

"Nancy," George looked surprised. "If Stacy

isn't letting Buttons out and Amanda isn't doing it either, there's only one suspect left."

"That's right," Nancy said confidently. "Mr. Johnson is letting Buttons out."

Mr. Johnson gasped. "No, I'm not!"

Nancy hurried to explain. "You aren't doing it on purpose." She looked over at Stacy. "Stacy, will you please tell Mr. Johnson the number one reason why Shetlands are like goats."

"Easy." Stacy folded her arms across her chest. "Shetland ponies can climb!"

"Oh my gosh!" Bess exclaimed. "Buttons has been climbing over the fence."

"Exactly," Nancy said as she walked over to the bale of hay near the fence. "Yesterday Scott climbed on the hay pretending to be a goat." Nancy stepped up on the bale. She swung one leg over the fence. "Stacy gave the final clue about Shetlands, and Bess and George reminded me about the first day we came to the petting zoo. There was a goat who had climbed on top of a bale of hay and was eating."

Nancy pulled herself over the fence, catching her back foot on the top rail as she leaped to the other side. For once, she didn't fall. She'd let her foot hit the fence rail on purpose, to prove a point.

"I get it." George clapped her hands. "The red paint was still wet when Buttons climbed

over the fence on his way to my house. Just like Nancy dragged her foot at the last minute, so did Buttons. He got paint on his hoof as he went over the fence."

"That explains the hay outside the fence, too," Bess added. "Buttons was kicking some of the hay over as he climbed out."

Nancy came around the petting zoo and back in the gate. "Mr. Johnson," she said, "I think Buttons doesn't like hay. If you want Buttons to quit running away, all you have to do is change the kind of food you give him." She paused, then added, "And when you put the hay in the pen for the sheep and goats at night, be sure to put it in the middle and not near the fence."

"Thanks," Mr. Johnson said. "You girls are good detectives." He immediately hurried over and dragged the half-eaten bale of hay to the center of the sheep and goat pen. "Do you think Buttons can climb out if I put it here?"

Nancy turned to Stacy. Stacy would know for sure.

"That looks like a good place," Stacy answered.

Mr. Johnson brushed a strand of loose hay from his hands, walked back under the shady area, then reached out and pulled his daughter in for a big hug. "I knew you were unhappy. I just didn't realize how bad it was," he told her. "Why didn't you tell me?"

Amanda simply shrugged.

"Well," Mr. Johnson said. "Now that I know, I think we should go to Hailey Town for a visit so you can see your old friends. Maybe we can go next week after school one day. Would you like that?"

Amanda nodded. "Thanks, Dad. I promise I'll try harder to make friends, and maybe then I'll like it better here in River Heights."

"We'd be happy to show you around," Bess chimed in. George and Nancy immediately invited Amanda to hang out on Saturday night. She agreed. They also asked Stacy. Stacy said she wanted to come too.

Plans made, Bess, George, and Nancy gave each other high fives.

"Case closed," Nancy declared.

❀ ❀ ❀

As a thank-you for solving the mystery, Mr. Johnson invited Nancy, Bess, and George to the petting zoo the following Saturday.

Mr. Drew drove the girls there. When they arrived, the zoo was crowded. There were people in the pen feeding the goats, sheep, chickens, and bunnies. A long line went around the outside of the fence wall. Lots of kids were waiting for a chance to ride Buttons.

The second he saw the girls, Mr. Johnson came over. "That article in the newspaper really worked." He waved his hand around the zoo. "Just look at how many people are here to see Buttons." Mr. Johnson pointed

over his shoulder to where his truck was parked. He'd changed the painted words on the outside of Buttons's trailer. It now read: JOHNSON'S PETTING ZOO. And beneath that: COME MEET BUTTONS, THE AMAZING CLIMBING PONY!

In fact, Mr. Johnson had made a special show for Buttons to appear in. Every hour, he set out a bale of hay inside the animal pen, right next to the fence. People would gather to see Buttons climb on top of the bale and leap over the fence.

Amanda was always waiting on the other side to give Buttons a piece of apple or carrot or some of the new pony feed they'd bought. No more hay for Buttons!

After the two o'clock show, Nancy, Bess, and George rushed up to Amanda.

"Are we still on for tonight?" Nancy asked.

"A movie, then a sleepover?" Amanda looked excited. "You bet! My dad will drop me off at your house after the petting zoo closes."

"I picked the movie," George said proudly. "It's about a girl and her pet pony." She grinned. "Of course, this girl's pony can't climb. It talks instead."

Everyone laughed.

"Stacy went to visit her grandparents again today," Nancy told them. "She'll meet us at the movie theater, then stay for the sleepover."

"I can't wait!" Amanda said good-bye before she hurried off to tell her dad all of their plans.

As they walked back to the car, Mr. Drew put his arm around Nancy. "I'm so proud of you." He winked at Bess and George. "I'm proud of the Clue Crew, too."

"We made new friends," Bess cheered.

"And we learned about Shetland ponies," George added.

Nancy looked over her shoulder at Amanda standing with her father. "It's amazing how many people one escaping pony brought together," Nancy said. Then, smiling, she added, "This mystery is all 'buttoned' up!"

Your own little horse . . . of course!

Do you wish you could have a pony of your own? Well, with the help of the Clue Crew, now you can! Nancy, George, and Bess found a way to design their own little ponies, and the best part is, you can keep them in the house!

First . . . saddle up these materials:

2 corks (Make sure one is bigger than the other one.)

6 toothpicks

Black, brown, or yellow yarn (You'll need only a little bit.)

Black or brown felt (Black or brown paper is okay too!)

2 black beads or googly eyes (or a black marker)

glue (any type)

Now trot along to these instructions:

Stick one toothpick into the large end of the bigger cork. Angle the toothpick upward to form the horse's neck.

Stick another toothpick into the small end of the bigger cork. Angle this toothpick downward to form the tail.

Give the pony legs by sticking four toothpicks in the bottom of the bigger cork. Using glue, attach strips of yarn to the pony's neck and tail. (This yarn is going to be the pony's mane and tail!)

Stick the large end of the smaller cork onto the pony's toothpick neck. If you have googly eyes or beads for the pony's eyes, you can glue them onto the smaller cork. But don't worry if you don't have any materials for eyes . . . just do what Nancy does! Take a black marker and draw some beautiful black eyes on the pony! (You can even give your pony eyelashes if you want to!)

Glue two small triangles of brown or black felt or colored paper on your pony's head for ears. If you want to dress your pony up, you can cut small pieces of felt or paper into the shape of a saddle and glue it onto the pony's back.

Congratulations! You have just created your own personal pony! Don't forget to give it a name!

HUNGRY FOR MORE MAD SCIENCE?

CATCH UP WITH FRANNY AS SHE CONDUCTS OTHER EXPERIMENTS!

Jump into history!
Read all the books in the

series!

#1 Lincoln's Legacy

#2 Disney's Dream

#3 Bell's Breakthrough

#4 King's Courage

#5 Sacagawea's Strength

Coming Soon:

#6 Franklin's Fame

A Cinderella with no glass slippers?

"I think we're rehearsing the ballroom scene," Nancy called out to her friends.

"I *love* that scene," Bess gushed. "It's so pretty!"

They got to the top of the stairs. Nancy expected to see all the students stretching at the barre and on the floor. But instead, everyone was huddled around Mr. McGuire. He looked very serious.

Andrea turned around and saw Nancy and her friends. She came running up to them. "Nancy! Bess! George!" she cried out. Her eyes were shiny with tears.

"Andrea, what's going on?" Nancy asked her curiously.

"My Cinderella slippers are gone," Andrea announced. "Somebody stole them!"

Nancy Drew and the Clue Crew™

#4

The Cinderella Ballet Mystery

By Carolyn Keene

Illustrated by Macky Pamintuan

Aladdin Paperbacks
New York London Toronto Sydney

CONTENTS

Chapter One: The Cinderella Ballet · · · · · · · · · 1

Chapter Two: Slippery Slippers · · · · · · · · · · · · · 12

Chapter Three: Missing! · · · · · · · · · · · · · · · · · · 20

Chapter Four: The First Clue · · · · · · · · · · · · · 28

Chapter Five: The Drama Queen · · · · · · · · · · · · 36

Chapter Six: A Blazing Headline · · · · · · · · · · 44

Chapter Seven: A New Suspect · · · · · · · · · · · · · 51

Chapter Eight: The French Clue · · · · · · · · · · · · 59

Chapter Nine: Bravo! · 70

CHAPTER ONE

The Cinderella Ballet

Nancy Drew slipped on her pink ballet shoes. "Let's stretch!" she said to her friends George Fayne and Bess Marvin.

George nodded. "Last one to the barre is a rotten egg!"

"Hey, not fair, you're closest to the barre!" Bess cried out.

The three friends hurried to the long wooden bar in front of the mirrored wall. Running was against the rules at Tim McGuire's Dance Studio, so they walked really, really fast instead.

The three girls had been taking lessons at Mr. McGuire's studio since the beginning of the school year. They were in the middle of rehearsing for a full-length ballet of "Cinderella." Opening night was on Saturday, only five days away.

Nancy got to the barre first, then Bess, then George. "Hmm, I wonder who's the rotten egg?" Bess joked.

George made a face. "Ha, ha."

Nancy put her right foot up on the barre with her toes pointed. She held onto the barre for balance. Then she curved her left arm over her head and leaned her body toward her right foot. Bess and George did the same. Nancy could feel the muscles in her right leg and the whole left side of her body stretching and getting loose.

Nancy glanced at the wall clock; it was five minutes before four. *Almost time for the rehearsal to begin,* she thought. The studio was filled with students who were busily putting on their ballet slippers or stretching.

Nancy noticed that Mr. McGuire was off in the corner talking on his tiny silver cell phone. His eyebrows were knit tightly together, and his mouth was pursed in a deep frown. Nancy thought that he looked upset. She wondered who he was talking to.

"Hey, Nancy Drew! I have a mystery for you," someone said.

Nancy glanced over her shoulder. Deirdre Shannon was standing there. Deirdre's best friend, Madison Foley, was standing next to her. They were dressed in identical shiny, purple leotards with matching supershort shorts, pink tights, and pink leg warmers.

"It's the mystery of the weird ballet outfit," Deirdre continued. "Did aliens come and dress

George Fayne in the middle of the night? Curious minds want to know!"

George was wearing a soccer T-shirt and shorts instead of a fancy leotard combo like Deirdre. Mr. McGuire didn't have strict rules about what to wear for rehearsals.

"You're so hilarious, Deirdre," George said. "Not!"

Deirdre cracked up. She looked over at Madison, who was searching through her dance bag for something, and poked her with an elbow.

"What? Oh!" Madison started cracking up too. Madison always did whatever Deirdre told her to do.

Nancy rolled her eyes and resumed stretching. She and her friends were used to getting all kinds of attention, even teasing, about the Clue Crew.

The Clue Crew was Nancy, Bess, and George's mystery-solving club. Their headquarters were located in Nancy's room. They stored their clues in one of Nancy's desk drawers. George kept track of their cases on Nancy's computer.

Just then, a boy named Gregory Auffredou came up to the girls. He was wearing a black T-shirt with the words "Dancing Fool" on it, black sweat pants, and black ballet shoes. He gave a friendly wave.

"Hi," Gregory said. "My mom made some chocolate chip cookies. Does anyone want one?" He reached into his dance bag and pulled out a plastic container.

"Yum! Thanks!" Bess plucked a cookie out of the container and bit into it. She began coughing and gagging. "Yuck! What is this?"

Gregory burst into laughter. "I got you!" he guffawed. "These cookies are totally fake. They're from my sister's toy kitchen."

Deirdre quickly took her digital camera out of her dance bag and snapped a picture. "I got you too Bess!" she giggled.

She held out the tiny screen on her camera for everyone to see. She had managed to get a picture of Bess's grossed-out expression and

the fake cookie hanging out of her mouth.

Nancy shook her head at Gregory. He always seemed to be playing practical jokes. Once he'd put fake worms in George's water bottle. Another time he'd put ice cubes in Madison's ballet slippers.

Bess handed the "cookie" back to Gregory. "You can have this back," she said huffily. She turned to Deirdre. "And you can delete that picture!"

"No way," Deirdre said with a grin. "I might

even post it on my website!" Deirdre had her own website, called Dishing with Deirdre. Her father had helped her set it up.

"Don't you dare!" Bess cried out.

Mr. McGuire clapped his hands. "Girls and boys! I want everyone on the floor. Now."

Nancy and her friends hurried over to the middle of the floor and sat down with their legs crossed. Deirdre, Madison, and Gregory sat down nearby.

The other students in the class included Nadine Nardo and Andrea Wu from River Heights Elementary School. There were also about a dozen kids who went to other schools. In "Cinderella," Gregory played the part of the prince. Deirdre and Madison were the wicked stepsisters. George was the wicked stepmother. Bess was the fairy godmother. Nancy, Nadine, and Andrea were mice who magically turned into Cinderella's coach drivers. They were also dancers and attendants at the prince's ball, along with some other kids.

The lead role of Cinderella was played by a girl named Autumn Gooden. Nancy glanced around. Autumn wasn't here yet. It wasn't like her to be late for class.

Scruffy, Mr. McGuire's golden retriever, came up to Gregory and gave him a kiss. For some reason, Scruffy loved to give Gregory wet, sloppy dog kisses. Nancy wondered if it was because Gregory often fed the dog cookies—*real* cookies—when Mr. McGuire wasn't looking!

Mr. McGuire sat down on his special blue director's chair in the front of the studio. "Hello, class," he began.

"Hi, Mr. McGuire," the class replied in unison.

Mr. McGuire had light brown hair and a slender, serious face. He used to be a professional ballet dancer. Nancy, George, and Bess had seen him in a production of *The Nutcracker* last year in Chicago. Nancy had loved the special holiday ballet, especially the second act, which was set entirely in the Land of Sweets. The stage had been filled with giant-size candies, cakes, and other goodies. Too bad those sweets were fake!

"I have some good news and some bad news," Mr. McGuire began.

Nancy, George, and Bess exchanged glances. *I wonder what the bad news is?* Nancy wondered.

"The good news is that all the costumes are now ready, thanks to Ms. Zelda's hard work," Mr. McGuire said. He smiled at Ms. Zelda, who was standing in the corner. Ms. Zelda was the costume manager. She nodded and waved.

"What's the bad news?" Deirdre asked.

Mr. McGuire's smile faded. "I just got a call from Autumn's mom," he said. "Autumn tripped on the stairs this morning and sprained her ankle. Fortunately, nothing's broken, so she's going to be fine in a couple of weeks. Unfortunately, she won't be able to dance the part of Cinderella."

Nancy gasped. Poor Autumn! She had been practicing so hard for her wonderful starring role. Now she wouldn't be able to be in the ballet at all.

"So who's going to be the new Cinderella?" a girl named Melanie asked him.

Mr. McGuire turned to Andrea, who was sitting in the back row. "Well, it only makes sense that Andrea should be the new Cinderella, since she's the understudy," he replied. Nancy remembered that an understudy was someone who learned a starring role in case he or she might have to be a substitute at the last minute.

"Yay!" Andrea squealed happily. "I mean, I feel really bad for Autumn. But I'm really glad I get to be Cinderella. And I already know all the dances!"

A boy named Rich who was sitting next to Andrea gave her a high five. Other kids congratulated her too.

Just then a pink ballet slipper came flying through the air. It hit the mirrored wall and fell to the ground.

Nancy recognized Nadine's shoe.

"That's not fair!" Nadine cried out.

Chapter Two

Slippery Slippers

Nancy stared at Nadine. Mr. McGuire had just named Andrea to be the new Cinderella. And Nadine wasn't taking it very well.

Why does Nadine always have to be such a drama queen? Nancy thought.

"Ms. Nardo, we don't throw shoes in the studio!" Mr. McGuire scolded her.

"It . . . was an accident," Nadine stammered.

"Yeah, right," Bess whispered to Nancy and George. "A likely story."

"Besides, why does Andrea get to be the new Cinderella?" Nadine went on. "*I* should be the new Cinderella!"

Nadine had tried out for the part of Cinderella

last month along with Autumn and Andrea. After the audition, Mr. McGuire had picked Autumn. Afterward, he had taken a long time to choose between Andrea and Nadine to be Autumn's understudy. In the end, he had gone with Andrea and made Nadine one of the mice instead.

"Andrea is my choice and that's final," Mr. McGuire said firmly to Nadine. "Now, let's get started with the rehearsal. First we'll run through the beginning of the ballroom scene. . . ."

"Hmph," Nadine protested. She didn't say anything more.

The students scrambled to their feet and took their places. Nancy was one of the dancers at the prince's ball, along with Nadine. As the fairy godmother, Bess was not in the scene. George, playing the wicked stepmother, would not be in the scene until later.

Mr. McGuire started playing the music on the CD player. Nancy's heart began racing. The music was so elegant and regal. She could almost imagine that she was at a royal ball in a beautiful castle in some faraway kingdom. She wondered what sort of pretty ball gown she would get to wear for this scene. Would it be purple, her favorite color? Or maybe blue?

"First position," Mr. McGuire called out. All the dancers put their heels together with their toes pointed out to the sides. They held their arms curved out in front.

"*Tendu* left and *glissade* stage right," Mr. McGuire said.

Nancy had finally gotten used to hearing the ballet steps called out in French. To do the *tendu,* she slid her left foot to the front, toes still pointed. Then she slid her foot to the side, then to the back.

For the *glissade,* Nancy glided over a few feet to the left. That was one of the most confusing things about ballet. "Stage right" meant go to the left. "Stage left" meant go to the right. It had to do with the audience's view, not the dancers' view. But it sure sounded backward to Nancy.

Still, the *glissade* was one of Nancy's favorite steps. It felt so light and breezy, as though she was dancing on air.

"Michael, don't lock your knees. Keep them loose. Nadine, other direction," Mr. McGuire said.

"Right, left, what difference does it make," Nadine said under her breath. Nancy was dancing close to her and could hear every word. "A terrible mistake has been made!" Nadine added.

"I'm sorry you didn't get to be Cinderella," Nancy whispered to Nadine as she did a *tendu* with her right foot. "But you're an awesome dancer! We need you in this scene."

"Hmph," Nadine said.

The group continued to rehearse the steps. Nadine kept muttering about how she should have been Cinderella.

Nancy couldn't help wondering: Was Nadine going to keep complaining about not being Cinderella? Was she going to make trouble for Andrea and the other dancers?

❀ ❀ ❀ ❀

"The Cinderella slippers have arrived!" Mr. McGuire announced.

It was Tuesday afternoon. Nancy, George, Bess, and the rest of the class were gathered in the studio for another rehearsal.

Nancy sat on the floor, pulling on her sky blue leg warmers, which matched her tights and leotard. She pulled her water bottle out of her bag and took a long drink.

"What Cinderella slippers?" Nancy asked the teacher.

"We ordered them from a very special store in Paris, France," Mr. McGuire explained. "They are for Autumn, I mean Andrea, to wear to the prince's ball. It's a lucky thing both girls wear the same shoe size. Ms. Zelda is downstairs now, getting the package from the deliveryman."

"Cinderella's glass slippers!" Bess whispered excitedly to Nancy and George.

Nancy nodded. She loved that part of the Cinderella tale.

In the story, Cinderella's fairy godmother

waved her magic wand and made Cinderella a special pair of glass slippers to wear to the prince's ball. She also turned Cinderella's raggedy dress into a beautiful ball gown, a pumpkin into a coach, and mice into coach drivers.

The fairy godmother warned Cinderella that she had to leave the ball by midnight because the magic spells would wear off then. Cinderella agreed. At the stroke of midnight, she left the prince's arms and rushed out of the ball. But in her haste, she lost one of her glass slippers. Later, the prince would comb the kingdom searching for her. He knew that whoever the tiny glass slipper fit must be his beloved princess.

"So Andrea has to dance in glass slippers?" George whispered to Nancy and Bess.

Nancy shrugged. "I don't know. She'd have to be really careful not to break them!"

Just then, Ms. Zelda came running out onto the studio floor. She was dressed in a silvery gray T-shirt and jeans. Her golden curls were piled on top of her head with fancy combs and pins. She was holding a white box covered with brightly colored stamps.

"The package has arrived from Paris!" she announced breathlessly. She had a soft voice with a French accent that sounded very sophisticated to Nancy.

"My Cinderella slippers!" Andrea exclaimed.

Mr. McGuire smiled. "Let's see them!"

Ms. Zelda started to open the box. She tried to rip the tape off. But it seemed to be stuck.

Gregory was standing next to Ms. Zelda. "You want some help, Ms. Z?" he asked her.

Ms. Zelda thrust the box at him. "*Oui,* that would be very kind."

Gregory took the box and began ripping. After a moment, he had the box open.

He reached in and pulled out a white shoe box with pink and silver stripes on it. He opened the lid and parted several layers of white tissue paper. Then he pulled out one of the glass slippers.

Nancy gasped. So did everyone else in the class. The slipper was beautiful! It was see-through and decorated with glittering, heart-shaped rhinestones. It looked very delicate.

Out of the corner of her eye, Nancy saw Deirdre get her camera out of her dance bag. She took a picture of Gregory holding the shoe.

"Deirdre, I told you before. No taking pictures during rehearsals!" Mr. McGuire called out.

Suddenly Gregory tossed the slipper in Andrea's direction.

"Catch!" he called out.

Startled, Andrea tried to catch the slipper—but missed.

Nancy gasped. Cinderella's beautiful slipper was about to hit the floor and break into a million pieces!

CHAPTER THREE

Missing!

Andrea screamed as the glass Cinderella slipper hit the hardwood floor.

But the slipper didn't break.

Gregory giggled. "What's the big deal? It's not real glass."

"Gregory!" Mr. McGuire said angrily. "Don't ever do that again!"

"What?" Gregory said innocently. "It was a joke."

"The slippers are not actually glass," Mr. McGuire explained to the rest of the class. "They're made of a certain kind of see-through plastic that looks like glass."

He glared at Gregory. "Still, never do that again. These slippers are from a very special store in Paris. If anything happened to them, we wouldn't be able to replace them in time for the show."

"Yes, Mr. McGuire," Gregory said. He hung his head sheepishly.

Andrea's face had turned ghostly white. She picked up the slipper and gave it back to Ms. Zelda. Ms. Zelda returned the shoe to the tissue-filled box. She frowned at Gregory and hurried away.

"Gregory's jokes are getting to be way too

extreme," George whispered to Nancy. Nancy nodded.

"Okay, that's enough excitement for today. Let's get started on the pumpkin coach scene," Mr. McGuire called out.

Everyone scrambled to their places, including Nancy. She closed her eyes for a moment so she could think about her part. The pumpkin scene was supertricky. On Saturday, during the real performance, she and Nadine would start the scene dressed in mice costumes. When Bess, the fairy godmother, waved her magic wand, the two girls would change into coach drivers.

In reality, Nancy and Nadine would hide behind some fake bushes for a second and slip out of their mice costumes. Underneath they would be dressed as coach drivers.

In the same scene, Andrea would change from a servant girl into a beautiful princess. Her costume switch was trickier. Nancy knew that Andrea would have to practice it lots of times before she got it just right.

"Here we go, everyone," Mr. McGuire said, clapping his hands. He turned on the CD player.

When the music began to play, Nancy pretended to be a little mouse. She curved her hands in front of her chest as though they were tiny paws. She began dancing lightly on her feet, like she was scurrying across the floor in search of cheese.

Nadine was right behind her, doing the same thing in exact time to the music. Bess was off in the corner, dancing merrily with Andrea.

Then Bess and Andrea crossed the floor with a series of graceful leaps. Just as they passed Nancy and Nadine, Nadine did a *tendu,* sticking her right foot out. Andrea tripped on Nadine's foot and fell to the floor!

"Ow!" Andrea cried out.

Mr. McGuire stopped the music. "What's going on?" he demanded.

"Nadine tripped me!" Andrea said. She sat up and brushed dust from her shorts and leotard.

"I did not!" Nadine protested. "It was an accident. I was doing my *tendu.*"

"You're not supposed to do a *tendu* there, Nadine," Mr. McGuire told her sternly. "You're supposed to do a plié."

Nadine shrugged. "Oh. Sorry."

Nancy frowned. Was Nadine telling the truth? Or had she tripped Andrea on purpose?

"Smile, everyone!"

Click!

Nancy whirled around. Deirdre was standing nearby, holding her camera. She had taken a picture of Andrea, Nadine, and Mr. McGuire.

"Nadine, could you get a little closer to Andrea?" Deirdre said, gesturing with her free hand. "This will be an awesome picture for my website."

"Deirdre!" Mr. McGuire exclaimed. "I told you that I didn't want any picture taking during rehearsals. Put that camera away. In fact, you're not allowed to bring it to rehearsals anymore. It's too distracting to the other dancers."

"Oh, baloney," Deirdre said. "I mean, okay. Whatever you say, Mr. McGuire." She walked over to her dance bag.

Andrea scowled at both Nadine and Deirdre. Then she stood up and got back into position.

Suddenly Deirdre let out a scream. "Ewwww-www!" she cried out.

"Now what?" Mr. McGuire sighed.

Deirdre made a face. "Someone put Silly Putty in my camera bag!" she announced.

"Gregory!" a bunch of kids cried at once.

"Gregory!" Mr. McGuire exclaimed too.

Nancy, George, and Bess exchanged a glance. With Nadine, Gregory, and Deirdre, today's rehearsal was turning into a three-ring circus!

"I hope Nadine isn't going to trip anybody today," Bess said.

"I hope Gregory isn't going to put anything yucky in anybody's dance bag today," George added.

"I hope Deirdre isn't going to be running

around with her camera today," Nancy piped up.

It was Wednesday after school. The three girls were on their way to Mr. McGuire's studio for another rehearsal.

Wednesday! Nancy thought. That meant there were only two more regular rehearsals—today and tomorrow—before the big dress rehearsal on Friday night. During dress rehearsal, all the dancers would be wearing their costumes and makeup.

And Saturday was opening night! Nancy's father, Carson Drew, would be there along with Hannah Gruen. Hannah was the Drews' housekeeper. But she was much more than that. Hannah had helped raise Nancy since she was three years old. That's when Nancy's mother had died. George's and Bess's families would be at the opening night performance too.

The three girls finally reached Mr. McGuire's studio. They ran up the stairs, their dance bags swinging from their shoulders.

"I think we're rehearsing the ballroom scene," Nancy called out to her friends.

"I *love* that scene," Bess gushed. "It's so pretty!"

They got to the top of the stairs. Nancy expected to see all the students stretching at the barre and on the floor. But instead, everyone was huddled around Mr. McGuire. He looked very serious.

Andrea turned around and saw Nancy and her friends. She came running up to them. "Nancy! Bess! George!" she cried out. Her eyes were shiny with tears.

"Andrea, what's going on?" Nancy asked her curiously.

"My Cinderella slippers are gone," Andrea announced. "Somebody stole them!"

CHAPTER FOUR

The First Clue

"What?" Nancy exclaimed. She couldn't believe the Cinderella slippers were missing.

"Who stole them?" George asked Andrea.

"We don't know," Andrea replied. She brushed a tear from her eye. "I can't dance on Saturday night without my glass slippers! What am I going to do?"

Nancy rushed up to the crowd around Mr. McGuire. He was talking to Ms. Zelda. Andrea, Bess, and George followed.

"Where did you put them, exactly?" Mr. McGuire was asking Ms. Zelda.

Ms. Zelda pointed to the storage area in the corner of the studio. Costumes hung neatly on metal racks. Shoes, hats, and other accessories were lined up on shelves.

"I . . . I put them over there last night, in their box," Ms. Zelda said. "The box is still there. But the slippers, they are gone! I have searched the whole studio three, four times. Oh, Monsieur McGuire, what are we going to do?"

Mr. McGuire turned to the sea of faces. "Does anybody know anything about this? Gregory?"

Maybe Mr. McGuire thinks this was one of Gregory's practical jokes, Nancy thought. *If it was, it's not very funny.*

"Who, me?" Gregory exclaimed, looking surprised. "I don't know anything. Honest!"

Mr. McGuire sighed. "All right. Ms. Zelda, please send an e-mail to the store in Paris and see if there's any way we can get a replacement pair sent by overnight courier. The rest of you, five minutes of stretches, then we'll start rehearsal."

Ms. Zelda bowed her head and hurried off. The students scattered around the floor and began their stretches.

Nancy, George, and Bess found an empty spot on the floor and sat down. Andrea sat down next to them.

"Hey," Andrea said in a low voice. "The three of you have a detective club, right? The Glue Crew?"

"The Clue Crew," Bess corrected her.

"Right. The Clue Crew," Andrea said quickly. "Can I hire the Clue Crew to find the missing slippers? I'll give you all my allowance for this week."

"You don't need to pay us," Nancy replied.

"Our club is all about being the best kid detectives ever. Not about making money," George added.

"And yes, we'll take your case," Bess piped up. She glanced at Nancy and George. "Um, if that's okay with you two."

Nancy and George nodded. Nancy felt a rush of excitement. She loved solving mysteries—even more than she loved dancing.

"We'll get on the case right away," Nancy told Andrea. "We'll do our best to find the slippers by Saturday."

George was busy rehearsing a scene with Deirdre and Madison. Nancy and Bess checked all the shoe boxes and accessory boxes on the shelves one more time. The missing slippers were nowhere to be found.

"This is so mysterious," Bess said as she picked

up yet another box and peered into it. "It's like they disappeared into thin air!"

"I know what you mean," Nancy said. "But they *have* to be somewhere. Things can't just disappear into thin air."

"I guess you're right," Bess agreed. "Slippers, where are you?" she called out.

Nancy sighed. The funny thing was, the box for the slippers was still there. It was on the shelf right where Ms. Zelda had left it last night. It was a pretty white box with pink and silver stripes and writing on the side.

"There's *got* to be a clue," Bess muttered. She picked up the pink and silver striped box and turned it upside down.

Just then, Nancy noticed something odd. Gregory was walking toward the storage area with Scruffy on a leash. Scruffy had his nose low to the ground, as though he was sniffing for something.

Gregory was looking at the ground the whole time too. In fact, he didn't even seem to notice Nancy and Bess.

That Gregory acts so strange sometimes! Nancy thought.

But Nancy's thoughts were interrupted by Bess's voice.

"Nancy!" Bess exclaimed. "I found something. I think it's a clue to the missing slippers!"

"I've never seen a barrette like that," George remarked.

Nancy sat cross-legged on her bed and leaned over to take a look. George was holding a silver barrette in the palm of her hand. It was zigzag shaped.

Bess had found the barrette at the dance studio, wedged into a crack in the shelf under the pink and silver striped shoe box.

George handed the barrette to Nancy. Then she moved over to Nancy's desk and started typing on the computer. This was one of George's jobs in the Clue Crew: entering and keeping track of the case on Nancy's computer.

"Clue: Zigzaggy barrette found under the

Cinderella shoe box," George read out loud as she typed.

"Do you think the slipper thief left it there by accident?" Bess suggested.

"Or maybe the barrette was there all along and doesn't have anything to do with the slipper thief," Nancy pointed out.

George typed all this into the computer.

Nancy turned the barrette over and over

in her hand. *It looks like a* Z, she thought. She turned it over again. *Now it looks more like an* N.

N—as in Nadine?

Did the barrette belong to Nadine? Nancy wondered. *Was Nadine the slipper thief?*

CHAPTER FIVE

The Drama Queen

Nancy held the barrette out to George and Bess. "At first I thought it was a *Z* shape," she said. She turned it sideways. "But now I'm wondering if it's an *N* shape."

"Maybe," George said.

Bess nodded slowly. She seemed to be following Nancy's train of thought. "That means it could be Nadine's! She wears barrettes."

Nancy leaned back against her pile of fluffy pillows and was quiet.

"Nadine was really, really mad that Andrea got to be Cinderella instead of her," Nancy said after a while.

George nodded. "It looked like she tried to

trip Andrea yesterday at rehearsal. But it might have been an accident."

"No way," Bess said. She grabbed a handful of buttery popcorn that Hannah had made for the girls. "That was *no* accident."

"So maybe Nadine stole the slippers to ruin the 'Cinderella' ballet for Andrea and everybody else," Nancy mused. "And while she was stealing them, her barrette fell and got stuck in the crack in the shelf."

George typed everything into the computer. "Let's look at it from a different angle. What if the barrette fell and got stuck there some other time? Like last week or last month or whatever?" she said out loud.

"Or what if the barrette belongs to somebody else with the initial *N*?" Bess added.

"I think we need to talk to Nadine as soon as possible," Nancy announced.

"I have to ask you something," Nancy told Nadine.

It was Thursday, a few minutes before rehearsal. The studio was already crowded with dancers who were stretching and getting ready. Nancy, Bess, and George had found Nadine in the corner by herself.

Nadine tugged her black leg warmers over her tights and glanced up at Nancy and her friends. "What?" she asked suspiciously.

Nancy pulled the silver barrette out of her dance bag and held it out to Nadine. "Is this yours?"

Nadine stared at the barrette. "Nope, that's not mine. Lately I only wear barrettes that are shaped like flowers, animals, or musical notes. That one is shaped like . . . well, I'm not sure what it's shaped like. It's either a lightning bolt or a really skinny tree."

"Actually, we think it's the letter *N*," George piped up.

"We? What do you mean, *we*? You're not on one of your crazy Clue Crew cases, are you?" Nadine asked.

"We are. We're trying to find the missing Cinderella slippers," Bess replied. "This barrette is a clue. A very *important* clue."

Nadine's jaw dropped. "Am I one of your suspects?" she demanded.

"Where were you between the end of Tuesday's rehearsal and the beginning of Wednesday's rehearsal?" Nancy asked her.

"Did you steal the slippers?" Bess blurted out.

"What made you do it, Nadine?" George added.

"I don't believe this!" Nadine exclaimed. "Of course I didn't steal those stupid slippers. Why is everyone so worried about them, anyway? Andrea can wear another pair of ballet shoes. *I'm* the real victim here. I was rejected for the part of Cinderella, not once, but twice!" She held up two fingers and stabbed them in the air dramatically.

"Maybe you stole the slippers because you're mad about not getting the part," Bess said.

"Of course I'm mad. I should have been

Cinderella!" Nadine huffed. "But why would I make things even worse by committing a crime? I don't want to spend opening night in jail!"

Nancy, Bess, and George exchanged a look. Nadine was being her usual drama-queen self. But was she telling the truth about not stealing the slippers?

Sometimes clues are a lot easier to figure out than people, Nancy thought.

On the studio floor, rehearsal was under way for one of the Act Two scenes. Nancy watched George, Bess, and some of the other dancers practicing pirouettes with Mr. McGuire's help. Pirouettes involved spinning on one foot and were difficult to do.

Nancy was not in this scene, so she took the opportunity to do a second search for clues. This time, she crawled around on the floor on her hands and knees to get a really close look. She peeked into every crevice. She peered into every nook and cranny. She found a lot of rusty bobby pins, empty paper cups, and dust bunnies. *Yuck,* she thought, making a face.

And then she found something a little more interesting in the set storage area. It was a small piece of white paper, half hidden under a shelf. She picked it up and stared at it closely. It said, "taille 35."

Nancy frowned. What did "taille" mean? Was that code for something?

Then she noticed that the words "taille 35" were written in the same fancy cursive style as the letters on the Cinderella shoe box. *Maybe the piece of paper came from inside the shoe box,* she thought.

It's definitely a clue, Nancy told herself.

She stuffed the piece of paper in her pocket and made a mental note to discuss it with her fellow Clue Crew detectives later. Then she brushed the dust off her tights and headed over to where her dance bag lay on the floor.

On her way, she almost tripped over Gregory's legs. He was sitting on the floor, going through his own dance bag. Scruffy was sitting next to him, sniffing everything.

Gregory moved his legs out of the way. "Oh, sorry," he mumbled.

Nancy glanced down. Gregory had dumped some of the contents of his dance bag out on the floor. There were some dirty socks, a water bottle, school notebooks, homework assignments, a half-eaten granola bar, dirty T-shirts, and a dirty towel. What a mess!

"Are you cleaning out your bag?" Nancy asked him curiously.

Gregory shook his head. "Nah. Just looking for something."

"Oh."

Nancy turned to go. But just then she noticed something shiny and glittery in the pile of Gregory's stuff.

It was a rhinestone. A small, clear, heart-shaped rhinestone.

It looked just like the rhinestones from the missing Cinderella slippers!

Chapter Six

A Blazing Headline

Nancy stared at the glittery, heart-shaped rhinestone lying among Gregory's things. It had to have fallen off one of the Cinderella slippers.

Did this mean that Gregory was the slipper thief?

"That looks like one of the rhinestones from the Cinderella slippers," Nancy said, pointing to the jewel.

Gregory stared at the rhinestone. His cheeks flushed red.

"That's not mine," he said quickly. "I don't know how it got there."

Nancy tried to figure out if Gregory was lying.

She couldn't tell. Still, he seemed to be hiding *something.*

"You don't know how it got there?" Nancy asked him.

"No way," Gregory said.

"It's definitely not yours?" Nancy persisted.

Gregory shook his head.

Nancy picked up the rhinestone. "Can I have it, then?"

"Sure," Gregory said with a shrug. "I don't want it."

Scruffy nuzzled his nose in Nancy's hand and sniffed the rhinestone. He began barking loudly.

"What's the matter, boy?" Nancy asked him.

Scruffy continued to bark at the jewel.

"Scruffy, be quiet!" Gregory said. He picked up one of his dirty socks and threw it across the floor. "Fetch, Scruffy!" he ordered.

Just then Nancy got an idea. While Gregory watched Scruffy fetch his sock, she leaned over and peeked into his dance bag. If Gregory was the slipper thief, the slippers might be in there.

But they weren't. All she could see was a paperback book, a magazine, and . . . a magnifying glass.

A magnifying glass? Nancy frowned. What was Gregory doing with that?

Scruffy had finally stopped barking and was chewing vigorously on Gregory's sock. Nancy turned to Gregory with a smile. "So why are you carrying a magnifying glass in your dance bag?" she asked him.

Gregory started. "Hey, what are you doing looking in my bag?" he demanded.

"It was open, and I just happened to—" Nancy began.

Gregory picked up his belongings and threw them into his bag. "You should stop poking around in other people's stuff," he said gruffly.

With that, he grabbed his bag and headed over to the barre.

❀ ❀ ❀ ❀

That night, the Clue Crew met at Nancy's house to go over their case. Nancy and Bess sat cross-legged on Nancy's bed while George sat at Nancy's desk.

"We have two new clues," Nancy announced.

She held out the heart-shaped rhinestone and the piece of paper that said, "taille 35." Bess and George studied them carefully.

"What does 'taille' mean?" Bess mused. "Did somebody misspell the word 'tail,' as in a doggy tail?"

"Maybe it's in code," George suggested.

"I wondered about that too," Nancy said. "In any case, I think it's definitely a clue because the letters are just like the fancy letters on the slipper shoe box."

George typed all this into Nancy's computer. "I know," she said suddenly. "Why don't I do a search for the word 'taille' on the Internet?"

"That's an awesome idea!" Nancy said eagerly.

George got on the Internet and typed in

a series of commands. After a moment, she glanced up from the computer. "It's a French word pronounced like 'tie,'" she announced. "It means 'size.'"

"Size?" Bess frowned. "So 'taille thirty-five' means size thirty-five?"

"I've never heard of a size thirty-five," Nancy said.

"Me neither," George said. "It sounds really, really big!"

George entered this new information into the computer. As she typed, Bess took the rhinestone from Nancy and examined it closely.

"It's so pretty," Bess said. Then she frowned. "If Gregory stole the Cinderella slippers and put them in his dance bag, the rhinestone could have fallen off one of the slippers."

"Or someone could have planted the rhinestone there to make him look guilty," Nancy pointed out.

George looked up from the computer. "We have three clues now: the barrette, the piece of paper with 'taille 35,' or size 35, on it, and the rhinestone heart," she reminded the other members of the Clue Crew. "The barrette doesn't exactly fit with Gregory being the thief."

"That's true," Nancy agreed. "Although Gregory sure owns a lot of weird stuff. Today I saw a magnifying glass in his dance bag."

"A magnifying glass?" Bess repeated. "Who does he think he is, Sherlock Holmes?"

Just then, a bell-like *ting!* sounded on Nancy's computer. George peered at the screen. "Andrea is instant messaging us," she announced.

"What did she say?" Nancy asked, leaning over.

"She says, 'Check out Deirdre's website right away,'" George read.

"Deirdre's website?" Bess repeated, looking confused.

George typed in the address for the Dishing with Deirdre site. Nancy and Bess got up from the bed and gathered around George.

The home page of Dishing with Deirdre filled

Nancy's computer screen. Across the top of it was the blazing headline WHO STOLE CINDERELLA'S SHOES?

"What!" Bess burst out.

"Typical Deirdre," George muttered.

Nancy reached forward for the mouse and used it to scroll down the page. Deirdre had written a "late-breaking story" about the theft of the Cinderella slippers from Tim McGuire's dance studio.

Then Nancy noticed something strange. Deirdre had included a photograph of the Cinderella slippers.

The slippers were lined up on a sidewalk in front of a brick wall.

What is wrong with this picture? Nancy asked herself.

Chapter Seven

A New Suspect

Nancy pointed to the photo. "Do you notice something really weird?" she asked her friends.

George and Bess stared at the photo. "N-no," George said after a moment.

"It's just a picture of the slippers," Bess said, shrugging.

Nancy stabbed her finger at the computer screen. "This photo was taken *outside,*" she explained. "How did Deirdre take a photo of the slippers outside?"

Bess gasped. "She must have taken the slippers from the studio!" she exclaimed.

George's eyes widened. "Maybe Deirdre is the slipper thief!" she said.

Nancy peered at the screen. “George, can you make this photo bigger?” she asked.

“No problem,” George said.

George’s fingers flew over the keyboard as she zoomed the photo to 150 percent, then 200 percent. “Is that big enough for you?” she asked Nancy.

Nancy nodded. “Perfect! Now, can you print it out?”

George went into the print menu and hit several keys. Nancy's printer whirred to life. A minute later it spit out a color copy of Deirdre's photo. The copy was twice the original size of the photo.

Nancy studied the printout. "None of the heart-shaped rhinestones are missing," she said after a moment. "That means this photo was taken *before* the rhinestone got into Gregory's bag somehow."

"Maybe Deirdre stole the slippers, then planted the rhinestone in Gregory's bag to make him look guilty," Bess suggested.

"Maybe," Nancy agreed.

"Deirdre's photo is an important clue," George said. "I have a feeling the Clue Crew is getting close to solving the case!"

"Yes!" Bess said, giving George a high five.

"I hope you guys are right," Nancy told her friends.

On Friday during recess, Nancy, George, and Bess found Deirdre on the swings. Madison was pushing her. The day was cool but sunny. A slight breeze stirred the leaves on the trees.

"Higher, higher!" Deirdre shouted to Madison.

Madison pushed Deirdre extra hard. Then she caught sight of Nancy and her friends and stopped.

"Madison, push!" Deirdre shouted.

"Uh, Deirdre? We've got company," Madison said.

Deirdre glanced down. She frowned when she saw Nancy and the others.

"Oh," Deirdre muttered. "*You* guys."

"Hello to you, too!" Bess called out cheerfully.

Deirdre dug her shoes into the dirt to slow down the swing. Dust sprayed up into the air. The swing came to a stop.

"Did you see the late-breaking story on my website?" Deirdre asked the girls with a sly smile.

"We sure did," Bess replied.

"It was a really interesting read," George added.

"And you had a really interesting photo to go with it," Nancy piped up.

Deirdre beamed. "Thanks! I took it myself, of course."

Nancy smiled. "Of course. Right *after* you took the slippers from Mr. McGuire's studio."

"More like *stole*," Bess said meaningfully.

"What made you do it, Deirdre?" George asked her.

Deirdre's cheeks flushed red. "What are you talking about? I'm not the slipper thief! I just took a photo, that's all," she insisted.

"Deirdre's totally innocent," Madison defended her friend. Nancy noticed that Madison kept her eyes on the ground, though. *Is she hiding something?* Nancy wondered.

"I think you guys are taking this Clue Crew stuff a little too seriously," Deirdre said, her tone turning mean. "I mean, it's not like you're real detectives or anything."

Nancy dug into her pocket and pulled out the folded-up computer printout. She unfolded it and held it up for Deirdre to see.

"Well, this is a *real* clue," Nancy said coolly.

"And according to this clue, you took this photo outside. Which means that you took the slippers from the studio."

Madison gasped. "Deirdre, we didn't think of that," she said, sounding panicked.

"Be quiet, Madison," Deirdre whispered.

"So you *are* the slipper thief," Nancy said to Deirdre. "Maybe you stole the slippers just so you could write a killer story about it for your website!"

Deirdre got up from the swing. She had a determined look on her face. "I am absolutely, definitely not the slipper thief," she said firmly. "All I did was . . . well, I kind of *borrowed* the slippers for, like, one or two seconds on Tuesday."

"What does that mean, 'borrowed'?" Bess asked her.

"I wanted to take a photo of the slippers for my website because they were so awesome looking and special," Deirdre explained. "But Mr. McGuire said I couldn't take photos in his studio because it bothered the other dancers or whatever. So I borrowed the slippers during a break. I took them outside, took the photo, and then brought them right back in. It was Madison's idea," she added.

"We didn't steal the slippers," Madison insisted.

"I thought Mr. McGuire said that you couldn't even bring your camera to rehearsals any longer," George said to Deirdre.

"He doesn't understand," Deirdre complained. "A reporter can't be without her camera!"

Nancy was thoughtful. "You took the photo on Tuesday," she said after a moment. "But you didn't post your story until Wednesday, after the slippers were missing. "

Deirdre nodded. "The whole thing was kind of a coincidence. I took the photo on Tuesday and posted it on my website Tuesday night. Ask anybody! Then on Wednesday, we all found out at rehearsal that the slippers had been stolen. When I got home that night, I wrote my excellent piece called, 'Who Stole Cinderella's Shoes?'

I posted it right away, next to the photo. I was really glad that I just happened to have the photo to go with the story."

Nancy considered this. Deirdre sounded like she was telling the truth. Or was she?

The bell rang, signaling the end of recess. "Gotta go," Deirdre said, waving at Nancy and the girls. "Good luck with your Crew Clue or whatever."

"Clue Crew!" George corrected her.

Deirdre ignored George. She turned and hurried through a crowd of kids toward the door. Madison followed close behind.

"Do we believe her?" Bess asked Nancy and George.

"I don't know," George replied, frowning in Deirdre's direction.

Nancy stuffed the printout of Deirdre's photo back into her pocket. "I don't know either," she said worriedly. "But I *do* know this: Tomorrow is opening night. We're running out of time!"

Chapter Eight

The French Clue

"It's the dress rehearsal, and I don't have any shoes to wear!" Andrea said, her eyes welling with tears.

It was Friday night. Mr. McGuire's studio was filled with the cast of the "Cinderella" ballet. Parents and other volunteers were busy helping the children on with their costumes or stage makeup.

"You can wear your pink ballet slippers for tonight," Mr. McGuire told Andrea. His cell phone began ringing. "Excuse me," he said, walking away to take the call.

Nancy was standing nearby, her mouse costume slung over her arm. She walked over to

Andrea. "It's going to be okay," she told Andrea. "The Clue Crew is going to keep looking for your Cinderella slippers until we find them!"

"I don't know," Andrea said doubtfully.

Nancy patted her dance bag. "We have those three clues I e-mailed you about: the rhinestone, the barrette, and the piece of paper with a French word on it. They're in my bag. We have some suspects, too. Don't worry, we'll find your slippers by tomorrow night."

"Okay," Andrea said. But she didn't look very sure.

One of the parents called Andrea over so she could style her hair. Andrea waved to Nancy and rushed off.

Nancy glanced around the room. Bess was getting sparkly eye shadow put on her eyelids by one of the volunteers. She looked so pretty in her fairy godmother costume, which was a glittery gold dress with a matching tiara.

George was on the other side of the studio, wearing her wicked stepmother costume: a long, dark gray dress with a high collar. Her eyebrows had been transformed into pointy, severe arches with a black eye pencil. Nancy thought George looked pretty scary!

"Can I help you on with your costume, Mademoiselle Nancy?"

Nancy turned around. Ms. Zelda was standing there. She had a box of safety pins in one hand and a sewing kit in the other. There was a long white tape measure draped around her neck.

"Thanks, Ms. Zelda, that would be great," Nancy said. Her mouse costume *was* kind of complicated.

Ms. Zelda led Nancy to a quiet corner of the studio. She took the mouse costume from Nancy and studied it carefully. "Why don't you sit on the floor and we can slip this on your feet first?" she suggested.

Nancy obeyed. Ms. Zelda tugged the mouse costume over Nancy's feet, which were covered with pink ballet tights.

"Hmm, maybe the mouse legs are still a little long," Ms. Zelda fretted. "I must pin them for you."

"Okay," Nancy said. "Thanks, Ms. Zelda."

As Ms. Zelda worked, Nancy looked around restlessly. She wished she could gather her Clue Crew around her and get back to work: searching for clues, interviewing witnesses, anything. But she knew this was dress rehearsal time. No matter how important it was to find the missing slippers, she, George, and Bess had to focus on their last chance to rehearse.

Ms. Zelda gave a big yawn. "Oh, *pardonnez-moi,*" she said, covering her mouth.

"Are you sleepy?" Nancy asked with a smile.

Ms. Zelda yawned again and nodded. "I have been working so hard here lately," she explained. "Sewing all the costumes, helping with the ticket sales, even designing the program. Oh, and a few nights ago Mr. McGuire asked me to help him move some old *Nutcracker* set pieces from the set storage area up to the attic, to make room. It was hard work—*tres difficile.* My muscles still ache from that."

Nancy sat up a little straighter. The set storage area? That was where she had found the piece of paper with the words "taille 35" on it.

Nancy reached over to get her dance bag. "Don't move," Ms. Zelda instructed her. "I must put one last pin in—there! Now you can move."

Nancy opened her dance bag and pulled out the "taille" clue. She showed it to Ms. Zelda.

"Do you know what this is?" Nancy asked her.

Ms. Zelda shrugged. "*Mais oui,* of course. It is a French shoe size."

"A shoe size? Isn't thirty-five kind of big for a shoe size? Maybe it's a shoe size for giants!" Nancy giggled at her own joke.

Ms. Zelda chuckled. "No, no. France is part of Europe. European shoe sizes are different. A European size thirty-five is about—oh, let us see, a size four for girls in America."

"Really?" Nancy exclaimed.

"Yes, really." Ms. Zelda looked amused. "Now, please stand up so I can check the rest of your costume."

Nancy got to her feet. Her mind was spinning. If taille 35 was the same as a girl's size 4, the piece of paper must have definitely fallen out of the box containing the Cinderella slippers. She remembered Andrea telling her once that she was a size 4.

Ms. Zelda bent over low to adjust Nancy's hemline. Just then Nancy noticed something. Ms. Zelda was wearing a shirt with the monogram *Z* embroidered on it in black.

Nancy cocked her head to the right. Sideways, the letter *Z* turned into the letter *N*. Could the silver barrette—one of the Clue Crew's clues—be a *Z* shape instead of an *N* shape, after all?

Nancy gave a little cough. "Um, excuse me, Ms. Zelda," she began. "Do you own a silver barrette?"

Ms. Zelda looked surprised. "*Oui!* But I seem to have lost it. I haven't seen it in several days."

She stared at Nancy. "Why do you ask?"

Nancy thought quickly. "I think I heard one of the other kids saying they saw something like that," she said. She wanted to hang on to her clue until she'd solved the case. "I'll ask around about it."

"Thank you, that's kind," Ms. Zelda said.

"Ms. Zelda, can you help me with my cape?" one of the other students called out. "It's too long!"

"Yes, yes, I'm coming," Ms. Zelda replied. She patted Nancy's costume, beaming. "There. You look just like a little mouse."

Nancy thanked Ms. Zelda as the older woman hurried away with her tape measure, safety pins, and sewing kit. Nancy gazed after her, wondering if the costume manager might be the slipper thief. But that didn't make any sense. Why would Ms. Zelda have stolen the slippers? Besides, Nancy didn't feel comfortable accusing her of being a thief. She was a grown-up, after all. Maybe Ms. Zelda lost the barrette, just as she said.

"Hey, Nancy Clue," someone said.

Nancy glanced up. Gregory was standing nearby. He looked handsome in his prince costume: black velvet pants and a royal white tunic with gold buttons.

"Hi, Gregory," Nancy said. She wondered if he had been eavesdropping on her conversation with Ms. Zelda.

Gregory pointed to the "taille 35" clue, which Nancy was still holding. "Where'd you get that?" he asked her curiously.

"In the set storage area," Nancy replied. "Why?"

"I want to show it to someone," Gregory said. "I'll bring it right back. Is that okay? I'll be supercareful with it."

Nancy thought for a moment. She wondered why Gregory *really* wanted to borrow the "taille 35" paper. Still, some instinct told her to say yes. Maybe she would learn something new and important about the case. After all, Gregory *was* a suspect.

"Sure," Nancy said with a smile. She handed the piece of paper to him.

"Thanks a lot!" Gregory said. Then he rushed off.

Nancy watched him as he hurried to the other side of the studio. She followed tentatively. Bess and George came up to her.

"You look so cool in your mouse clothes!" Bess exclaimed.

"You guys look really great in your costumes too," Nancy said. She lowered her voice. "I'm following Gregory."

"Why?" George asked.

Nancy explained. "I want to know what he's going to do with the 'size thirty-five' clue," she finished.

"We're all dressed and we have our makeup on," Bess whispered. "We have about twenty minutes until the first scene. We can help you!"

Nancy nodded. She put her finger to her lips. Then she, George, and Bess began following Gregory again.

The studio was bustling with activity, so Gregory didn't seem to notice that he was being watched. He walked toward Scruffy, who was curled up in the corner on an old red blanket.

Gregory bent down next to Scruffy and held the piece of paper Nancy had given him under the dog's nose. Scruffy sniffed. Gregory said something to him. Then Scruffy got up and began walking this way and that, his nose low to the ground, continuing to sniff.

"What is Gregory doing?" George whispered to Nancy.

"What is *Scruffy* doing?" Bess added.

Nancy frowned. *What* are *they doing?* she wondered.

Then something occurred to her.

"On Wednesday I saw Gregory walking around the set storage area with Scruffy," Nancy said out loud to her friends. "It's like he was using Scruffy to help him find something. Then yesterday, when I found the rhinestone in Gregory's stuff, Scruffy started sniffing it and barking like crazy."

Bess and George both stared at her. "What do you think all that means?" George asked her.

Nancy's eyes flashed. "I think I know what happened to the Cinderella slippers," she announced.

CHAPTER NINE

Bravo!

George gasped. "You know what happened to the slippers?" she demanded. "What? Who? Where? How? Why?"

"I think Gregory is the person who should be answering those questions," Nancy said.

Nancy marched up to Gregory and Scruffy, with George and Bess at her heels. Gregory stopped and turned around. Scruffy gave a short bark.

Nancy put her hands on her hips and stared sternly at Gregory. She felt a little silly doing that in her mouse costume. But this was important.

"You took the Cinderella slippers, didn't you?" Nancy accused Gregory.

Gregory's cheeks turned bright red. "Uh, n-no way," he stammered. "I d-don't know what you're talking about."

Bess stepped up. She put her hands on her hips too. "You *do* know," she said. "And you'd better tell us!"

Gregory stared at the floor. Scruffy barked at him.

"I think you took the Cinderella slippers on Tuesday, as a joke," Nancy guessed. "You hid them somewhere, maybe in the set storage area. Then you forgot where you hid them. Or someone moved them. Either way, now you don't know where they are. You've been looking for them since Wednesday, using Scruffy's super-duper doggy nose."

Bess seemed to pick up on Nancy's thoughts. "You let Scruffy smell the rhinestone and the piece of paper with the size on it to help track down the slippers," she said slowly.

Gregory looked up and stared at her, his eyes wide. "How'd you guys know all that?" he asked her.

"That's why we're the Clue Crew," George said with a grin.

"Oh." Gregory frowned. "I didn't mean to steal the slippers, exactly," he confessed finally. "I was just going to hide them, as a joke, like

Nancy said. I did it after rehearsal on Tuesday."

"Is that the last time you saw them?" Nancy asked him.

Gregory nodded. "On Wednesday, when Andrea and everyone else figured out the slippers were missing, they all freaked out! I thought that was kind of funny. Then I went over to the hiding place to get them. But they were gone!"

"Where did you get the rhinestone?" Bess said.

"It fell off on Tuesday when I hid the slippers," Gregory replied. "I was going to glue it on later. I let Scruffy smell it so he'd help me find the slippers. He has an awesome sense of smell. I think his great-grandfather was a bloodhound."

Then something else occurred to Nancy. "That's why there was a magnifying glass in your dance bag," she said suddenly.

"Yeah. I was trying to act like a real detective so I'd solve the mystery," Gregory admitted. "I guess it didn't work. The slippers are still gone. Mr. McGuire is going to be supermad at me." He sighed unhappily.

Nancy thought for a moment. "Where did you hide the slippers on Tuesday?" she asked him.

"In a giant ice-cream sundae," Gregory replied.

"A giant ice-cream sundae?" Nancy, George, and Bess repeated in unison.

Gregory nodded. "Yeah. It was made of painted wood. It had a little shelf on the back part of it. I put the slippers there. But then the whole thing disappeared! Like, how did *that* happen?"

Nancy gasped. It all made sense now.

"I know where the sundae is!" she exclaimed.

"You do?" Gregory asked her eagerly. "Where? I'll give you my magnifying glass if you find the sundae," he offered.

"You can keep your magnifying glass," Nancy told him. "Come on, guys, we have to get up to the attic!"

"The attic?" Bess said, sounding confused.

"The giant ice-cream sundae is from *The Nutcracker,*" Nancy said, heading for the stairs.

Bess, George, and Gregory followed Nancy. The four of them raced up the stairs to the attic. Scruffy bounded behind them.

Nancy had never been in the attic before. It was a big room with a ceiling that sloped down on either side, following the lines of the roof. It was full of set pieces and props: giant trees, the fronts of buildings, fake lampposts, Victorian furniture. Everything was covered with a fine layer of dust. Scruffy sneezed; so did Bess and George.

"Okay, what's this about *The Nutcracker*?" George asked Nancy as she sneezed again.

"Ms. Zelda told me that she moved some old set pieces from *The Nutcracker* from the studio up to the attic, to make room," Nancy explained breathlessly. "This was Tuesday night. "

"Tuesday night?" Gregory cried out. "That's right after I hid the slippers."

Nancy nodded. "Exactly! Now, we just have to find the giant ice-cream sundae somehow. There's an awful lot of stuff here."

"And we can't mess up our costumes, or Mr. McGuire will *really* be mad," George pointed out.

"And we don't have a lot of time," Bess said.

But it took Nancy and her Clue Crew only a few minutes to find the giant ice-cream sundae. It had been shoved in between a huge cookie and an enormous piece of pie.

Nancy peered behind the sundae. She saw the shelf Gregory had mentioned. Actually, it was more like a little nook.

The Cinderella slippers were there!

Nancy pulled them out and held them up in the air. "Yay, we found them!" she exclaimed.

"The Clue Crew does it again," George said with a big grin.

Nancy stood behind the blue velvet curtain. She peered through a crack between two curtain panels. "Oh, I see Dad and Hannah," she said excitedly. "They're sitting in the front row!"

"I see my parents," Bess said.

"I see mine, too," George added.

It was opening night. The curtain would go up in a few minutes. Backstage, everyone was buzzing with excitement. Ms. Zelda hurried around making sure everyone's costumes were on just right. Mr. McGuire rushed here and there, checking that the lights and sound equipment were working properly.

Andrea came up to Nancy and her friends. She was dressed in her Act I Cinderella clothes: a simple gray dress, black tights, and black ballet slippers. In Act II, she would be transformed into a beautiful princess with her long pink ball gown—and of course, her special Cinderella slippers.

Andrea gave each of the three girls a big hug. “I don't know how to thank you guys,” she said happily. “You really *are* the most awesome detectives in the world!”

“I'm just glad we found your slippers in time for opening night,” Nancy said.

“Gregory apologized to me and Mr. McGuire,” Andrea said. “He brought us both homemade cookies from his mom too. They were real this time.” She giggled.

“That's good.” Nancy giggled too.

“Places, everybody!” Mr. McGuire announced in a loud whisper. “Curtain in two minutes.”

“Oh, my gosh!” Bess exclaimed.

Nancy and her friends ran to their places. Nancy's heart was pounding so hard that she thought it would burst out of her chest. It was opening night! And she was in the show! She was not just a real detective but a real ballerina, too.

The lights in the theater dimmed. The music began to play.

The blue velvet curtain closed after the final act. Applause rang out in the auditorium.

Behind the curtain, the dancers rushed around, looking for their places to take a bow. Nancy bumped into George.

"Ow, sorry!" Nancy giggled.

"Wasn't that *awesome*?" George said breathlessly.

Bess ran up to them. "That was so much fun," she said. "I think we should all be dancers when we grow up!"

"Dancer-detectives," George said, nodding. "We'll solve mysteries during the day and dance on stage at night!"

Mr. McGuire stepped out from one of the stage wings. His usually serious-looking face was glowing with excitement. "Places, everyone!" he said in a loud whisper. "It's time to take your bows."

"I can't believe it's over!" Bess gasped.

Nancy took her place. So did George, Bess, and the other dancers. After a few seconds, the curtain swished open. Nancy was dazzled. Her eyes took a minute to focus because the stage lights were so bright, and the auditorium was dark.

Everyone was clapping like mad. Nancy tried to make out her father and Hannah in the audience. She finally spotted them. Her father was holding a bouquet of flowers and a big stuffed teddy bear. They were for Nancy!

Then Mr. Drew and the whole audience stood up. This was a standing ovation, which meant that the people really, really liked the ballet.

Nancy took her bow along with the other dancers. After a moment, Andrea swept out from the wing of the stage and took a special bow, since she was Cinderella. The crowd clapped even more loudly. Andrea looked so pretty. Her Cinderella slippers glittered brightly under the stage lights.

The curtain closed, then opened again. The audience just kept clapping. Nancy turned to look at George and Bess and grinned. They grinned back.

The Clue Crew had done it again!

Nancy, Bess, and George's Ballerina Finger Puppets

Nancy, Bess, and George love to put on a show of their own with these cute ballerina finger puppets. You can too!

You will need:

White posterboard
Pencil
Scissors
Markers
Construction paper or
  wrapping paper
Glue
Fabric scraps
Colored (not clear) fingernail polish
Glitter, small rhinestones (optional)

*Draw the outline of a ballerina on the posterboard with the pencil. Just draw the ballerina's head, torso, and arms—no legs. Her head and torso together should be about as tall as the length of your hand from your wrist to your knuckles. Her arms can be posed like ballerina arms—out to the side, over her head, or one arm up and one arm to the side. You decide!

*Cut out your ballerina shape with the scissors. Near the bottom of the torso, cut out two legholes for your fingers to go through. (Your fingers will be the ballerina's legs!)

*Use the markers to draw her eyes, nose, and mouth. You can make her smiling or serious—or even mean-looking, like Cinderella's wicked stepmother!

*Use the construction paper or wrapping paper to create her hair and leotard. Sketch the hair and leotard with the pencil, then cut them out with scissors, and glue them onto your posterboard ballerina. Another option: You can use markers to draw her hair and leotard instead.

*Use the fabric scraps to create her tutu (which is a fancy French word for a ballet skirt). Cut a triangle shape that would be the right size for a skirt; then trim one corner of the triangle so it can be her waist. Glue the tutu onto your posterboard ballerina.

*If you want, you can glue glitter or small rhinestones onto her leotard or tutu (or even her hair).

*Paint the fingernails of your middle finger and the finger next to your thumb with a pretty color. Those will be your ballerina's toe shoes! When your fingernails are dry, put those fingers through the two legholes in your ballerina's torso.

It's Time to Dance!

Drape a pretty scarf or other cloth over a table, the back of a chair, or other hard surface for your ballerina's "stage." Then put on a CD of classical music like *The Nutcracker* by Tchaikovsky or *A Midsummer Night's Dream* by Mendelssohn—or whatever music you and your ballerina feel like grooving to.

The More the Merrier

Invite your friends over to make ballerina finger puppets with you. Then you can all put on a show together! If you want to make finger puppets from the Cinderella ballet, you can use these instructions to make a fancy Cinderella, a fairy godmother, or even mice!

How Did They Do Leaps and Jumps in THAT?

In the early days of ballet, dancers' skirts came all the way down to the floor. But eventually, dancers wanted costumes that would show off their steps and make it easier for them to move around. In the early 1700s, dancers started wearing ballet skirts above their ankles. Over the next three hundred years, the ballet skirts continued to get shorter and shorter.

Read all the books in the

Blast to the Past

series!

#1 Lincoln's Legacy

#2 Disney's Dream

#3 Bell's Breakthrough

#4 King's Courage

#5 Sacagawea's Strength

#6 Ben Franklin's Fame

Coming Soon:

#7 Washington's War